T0142577

Battered FAITH

Tanya South

WESTBOW
PRESS®
A DIVISION OF THOMAS NELSON
& ZONDERVAN

Scriptures taken from the Holy Bible, New International Version®, NIV®. Copyright © 1973, 1978, 1984, 2011 by Biblica, Inc.™ Used by permission of Zondervan. All rights reserved worldwide. www.zondervan.com The "NIV" and "New International Version" are trademarks registered in the United States Patent and Trademark Office by Biblica, Inc.™

WestBow Press books may be ordered through booksellers or by contacting:

WestBow Press
A Division of Thomas Nelson & Zondervan
1663 Liberty Drive
Bloomington, IN 47403
www.westbowpress.com
1 (866) 928-1240

Because of the dynamic nature of the Internet, any web addresses or links contained in this book may have changed since publication and may no longer be valid. The views expressed in this work are solely those of the author and do not necessarily reflect the views of the publisher, and the publisher hereby disclaims any responsibility for them.

Any people depicted in stock imagery provided by Thinkstock are models, and such images are being used for illustrative purposes only. Certain stock imagery © Thinkstock.

ISBN: 978-1-5127-9991-0 (sc)
ISBN: 978-1-5127-9992-7 (hc)
ISBN: 978-1-5127-9990-3 (e)

Library of Congress Control Number: 2017913079

Print information available on the last page.

WestBow Press rev. date: 08/21/2017

CONTENTS

ACKNOWLEDGMENTS

MY FIRST AND deepest gratitude is to the Almighty Creator of heaven and earth, our God, who is in complete control of our lives. He individually creates and writes each of our own unique life stories. He's blessed me to experience countless happy moments and has sustained me through the experiences of suffering during many dark days. But no matter how dark those days were, the good news is, He is also the perfecter and finisher of my faith, of my story. All of our life stories stand out in their own way. God has placed within me the gift and idea to write this story. He's blessed me with more than I deserve. I thank Him for every single thing in my life.

I thank Him for the wonderful family He's given to me. I am grateful for my loving husband, who supported me throughout my writing journey. Through all of the days and long nights I stayed up late writing, he never complained. With all of the interruptions of me reading to him and asking him what he thought about each chapter, no matter what he was doing or working on, he would always stop to listen or give me advice. I thank God for blessing me with my other half, who's a gift and always supports me and my dreams. I love you, James!

I am also thankful for our four beautiful children, Caiden,

Cameron, Zabrina, and Jimmy. You are the air that I breathe and the hearts of my soul. I love you with everything that's inside of me. You are the four greatest gifts God could ever give to me. Thank you for believing in me.

Thank You for my loving mom, Sonia, for teaching me about faith and love in how she lives her life as an example to me and our family. She taught me to trust in the Lord. She is a wonderful gift to me. Thank You for also encouraging me to keep writing. I love you, Mom!

PROLOGUE

But each person is tempted when they are dragged away by their own evil desire and enticed. Then, after desire has conceived, it gives birth to sin; and sin, when it is full grown, gives birth to death. Don't be deceived, my dear brothers and sisters.

—James 1:14–16 (NIV)

AS THE SUN finally lay down to rest and the purplish-pink clouds slowly disappeared, it quickly grew dark. The deep black sky was perfectly painted with a splash of tiny, bright diamond-like specs. It looked like a perfect piece of art that God had carefully put together, the finest ever seen by humankind. The night was completely still. A sudden swirl of loud sirens disrupted that peaceful evening. Two police cars rushed in. The blinding bright blue and red lights strobed fast and looked like July fireworks in December. Raymond's eyes filled with shock, confusion, and disbelief.

"Don't move! Hands behind your head!" she said.

"Whoa! What? Are you a cop? ... I was just—" he said.

"Be quiet! Hands behind your head!" the female detective shouted while she pointed her P226 black Sig pistol at him.

She quickly and firmly grabbed Raymond's arms, pulled them

behind him, and placed the cold, hard handcuffs on him. They clicked around his wrists.

"Ahhhh, that hurts!" he yelped. "Please, give me a chance … I've never done this before."

Raymond wondered who this female was, speaking with sudden authority. She was dressed in a tight black minidress, which hung slightly off the shoulder, and black lace stockings. She had velvety red lips.

"Are we role playing?" Raymond said and laughed.

But it was apparent that the woman didn't find it amusing. *Wait.* It now occurred to him that she must have been an undercover cop. Raymond felt his world quickly fracture, and the pieces of it crumbled all around him like glass that had been pummeled with a hammer. As his rights were being read to him, the sound of the detective's voice echoed like words being spoken in a dark tunnel. The words faded away like echoes from a far distance. Raymond's body grew cold, and droplets of sweat streamed down from his forehead onto his eyebrows. His heart sprinted fast and pounded, and his body trembled. He looked up at the thick glass in front of him. He realized then that he sat in the back of a police car.

"How can this be happening? I'll just tell Melissa that I was at the wrong place at the wrong time," Raymond whispered to himself.

It was obvious that the wheels were turning in his head from the look on his face. Raymond's thoughts tripped over each other as he worked hard to think up the most believable lie. Raymond was a good liar. It was easy and second nature for him. He'd gotten away with it so many times before, using his charm and wit. It looked like his charm had run out this time. Finally, the car pulled up in front of the precinct. Raymond was yanked from the backseat.

"Hurry up! Let's go," the detective said.

When Raymond walked in, he saw what appeared to be a woman, but not everything was as it seemed. It was a man dressed like a woman. He was wearing heavy makeup, including greenish-blue eye shadow and bubblegum-pink lipstick, and a long black wig. The man's eyes were glued to Raymond.

"Hey, love, want me to show you a good time?" the man said as he winked at him.

Raymond was then walked over to sit on the next bench.

"What was I arrested for?" Raymond presumptuously asked.

"You know exactly why you were arrested! You were arrested for solicitation."

"Solicitation?" Raymond asked.

"Yes, of prostitution. You do know what that is, right? Just cut it out!" the detective said.

Raymond entreated the officer, "Please don't tell my wife! I have a one-year-old daughter, and my wife is six months pregnant. This won't be good. Please! Christmas is in two days. I really need to be with my family," Raymond begged.

"I'm sorry. Tell it to the judge. You should have thought about that before," the female detective said as she shook her head in obvious disgust.

In an eight-by-eight cell, Raymond sat on the bench, bent over his lap with his hands on his head.

"What am I going to do? What in the world is wrong with me? I'll just tell Melissa I was arrested for disorderly conduct, or better yet, driving while intoxicated."

Raymond leaned his head back against the wall and looked up at the ceiling. He had a quick memory from just a few months before when his wife, Melissa, began getting herself and baby Sarah ready to attend Sunday worship at their local gospel church. He thought back.

"I just dressed the baby … I've tried on just about everything I own … and the clothes all fit me tight. I'm only eight weeks along, ugh. What about you, Raymond? Why aren't you getting dressed?"

"Ahh, leave me alone … You know I can't stand that worship nonsense. Besides, there are so many hypocrites in church. You go ahead with Sarah. I'm going to meet up with a couple of the guys and play ball," Raymond said.

"Raymond!" Melissa entreated him. "The last time you came to church with me was on Easter Sunday. As far as hypocrites going to church, you shouldn't be concerned with other people and what they are doing; it's about our own personal relationship with the Lord."

"Relationship with the Lord?" Raymond laughed. "See, there you go again with that nonsense. Well, I guess I don't want to have a relationship with *the Lord*!" Raymond said in a mocking manner. "Where was the Lord when my dad abandoned me and my mom? Where was He when we were struggling and sometimes had barely any food to eat? How about when our apartment was a revolving door for different men that my mom had? There was George, Tim, Pete, and all other ones. I can't remember their names … A couple of them, by the way, would beat me and my mom too. And my own mother couldn't even protect me. So please, Melissa, don't talk to me about your Lord, 'cause He was never around for me!"

"What is the matter with you?" Melissa walked away from him and continued getting herself ready.

"Don't walk away from me like that? Who do you think you are? Get over here!" Raymond shouted.

"Please, not now, Raymond. Don't do this. It's okay. You do what you want. I'm sorry that I even said anything."

As she began to walk into their bedroom, Raymond stormed

behind her. Melissa's head suddenly jerked back. She realized at this point that Raymond had yanked her from the back of her head. He grabbed a tight hold of her long, dark-brown hair.

"Raymond! Stop!"

"Woman! I told you to come to me! Don't you ever walk away from me again!" Raymond pulled her with force as he subdued her. He turned back around to walk out while still holding her hair.

His face displayed deep rage. Melissa cried loudly. She fell to the ground as he dragged her across the floor into the living room. Little Sarah was only almost six months old. She sat in her high chair and had no real idea of what was happening to her mama. She began crying out of fear from her mother's bloodcurdling cries.

"Get up!" shouted the officer.

The harsh reality brought Raymond back to his present nightmare as he sat in the cold, filthy jail cell.

When Jesus Christ was on this earth, He healed the sick, raised the dead, cast out demons, restored the broken, and redeemed the ashamed. Jesus said, "Come to me all who are weary and burdened, and I will give you rest." Melissa's spirit was broken and weary. She hung on to every word of this truth, but her faith and spirit, like her physical being, continued to be battered. She didn't realize that when she married Raymond, she had entered a world of madness. It was going to take her all the faith she had inside of her to get through the most excruciating storm of her life.

CHAPTER 1

God Will Provide

Look at the birds of the air; they do not sow or reap or store away in barns, and yet your heavenly Father feeds them. Are you not much more valuable than they? Can any one of you by worrying add a single hour to your life? And why do you worry about clothes? See how the flowers of the field grow. They do not labor or spin. Yet I tell you that not even Solomon in all his splendor was dressed like one of these. If that is how God clothes the grass of the field, which is here today and tomorrow is thrown in the fire, will he not much more clothe you— you of little faith?

—Matthew 6:26–30 (NIV)

THE TIE-DYED MORNING sky swirled with deep blueish, coral-tinted clouds. The fiery sun peeked over the rooftops of the buildings. Fire-truck sirens were piercing, almost deafening. The car horns ferociously honked, and the noise of busy traffic filled the room. The busy streets in Bronx, New York, were buzzing as usual. The window was opened ever so slightly. On the other side of the glass, there were long cooing sounds and sudden flapping wings. The pigeon continued to peck at the steel window frame. There was a hint of car exhaust, and scents of the street crept in. Melissa awoke to her environment's natural alarm clock. Her eyes opened up to the sight of a dark yellowish-brown ceiling, which was crackling because of the leak that had started just a few days ago. She walked over to her toddler's bed to find her sitting up, babbling and smiling.

"Good morning, baby," Melissa said to her one-year-old, Sarah. Melissa's belly fluttered with light rolls under her skin.

She peeked down to her perfectly round belly with her very active baby moving inside of her. She was six and a half months pregnant with her second baby. She thanked the Lord.

"Thank You, God, for my gifts. Thank You for another day."

Finally, after she finished the morning tasks of feeding and dressing little Sarah, Melissa got ready to go to work. After dropping Sarah off at the sitter's, Melissa went on her way to catch the six train from the Bronx to Manhattan. She entered the station to the commotion of people everywhere. Approaching the turnstile to swipe her metro card was a task, as she had to walk past the herd of people who would shove just about anyone out of the way to make their train. Then, she had to walk up the lengthy four flights of steps to the platform, which was another tedious task. It was a polar-opposite scene on the platform. Everyone was mostly quiet. Some were wearing their headphones; others were texting on their cell phones. The loud, swooshing silver train pulled in, and the herd of people rushed in. Melissa waddled in carefully through the opened doors.

The express train was then going about fifty miles per hour. As she stood there for about ten minutes with her very visible round belly, she stared out into the black tunnel; right in front of her sat a nurse, wearing her uniform and reading her newspaper. The nurse took a quick glance and peeked around the corner of her paper. She looked up at Melissa and quickly resumed reading her newspaper. Melissa was still standing; her back was hurting and her elephant-like ankles were swollen from having edema during the middle part of her pregnancy.

Melissa thought, *God, please let me make it to work okay.*

The lights on the train seemed to be getting darker, flickering on and off. She was sweating as if she had just run a marathon. Her hands were clammy, and her heart was beating hard and fast. She looked over to the man standing next to her to let him know she felt faint.

"Sir … I think …" *Boom!* Melissa fell to her knees and back onto the crowd of people.

There were loud sighs that buzzed in the air. The man standing beside her swooped her up and asked the nurse and two other people to get up so he could lay her down.

"Can't you see that this woman is pregnant? Can you please get up?"

Then the train arrived at the 125th Street stop in Manhattan.

The conductor announced everyone was to evacuate the car. "Everyone, please exit the train. Please exit the train … We have a sick passenger."

The EMTs rushed in, picked Melissa up, and laid her on a stretcher.

Melissa awoke, confused and in a panic. "What happened? Did I just pass out? I really need to get to work."

The emergency medical technician said, "Miss, I don't think that's a good idea." When he took her blood pressure and temperature, he said, "Your blood pressure is a little low. Are you anemic?"

As she nodded, she said, "Yes, I am but have only been so during my pregnancy. I've been taking iron supplements for that. Can I please have some water?"

They gave her a fresh cold bottle of water. She got up and insisted that she was fine.

"I'm okay ... I'm okay. I just really need to get to work," Melissa insisted.

"Miss, we suggest that you go to the hospital. If not, you really need to follow up with your doctor," the EMT said.

"I need to call my husband."

Melissa tried calling her husband from the public telephone in the station because her cell phone had no signal, but he didn't answer.

"Are you sure you don't want to go to the hospital instead?" the EMT asked.

"No, I'm fine. Thank you so much for your help."

Melissa found a small bench to sit on. The air was cool and stale with a hint of garbage. The platform was engaged with entertainment. On one end, three teens were break dancing with an empty bucket to collect any money after their performance. At the other end of the platform stood an older man with threaded white hair, wearing an old, beat-up hat, playing a saxophone version of the "New York, New York" tune. Next to Melissa was a mother with her young son, cradling him in her arms. It reminded Melissa of Sarah, and she anxiously wanted to get home to her little girl. Worrisome thoughts invaded her mind. As a result of her fainting spell, she knew that she had to follow up with her midwife the next morning.

The Following Day

The midwife, Sandra, said, "Well, sweetheart, I don't want to alarm you—"

"Is everything okay?" interrupted Melissa.

"The baby is fine, but your cervix is one centimeter dilated."

"What does that mean?" Melissa asked.

"Well, you're in danger of going into labor prematurely, which puts the baby at risk," Sandra explained. "The good news is I am putting you on bed rest for the rest of your pregnancy. You just need to take it easy."

"Oh no! What do you mean? My baby, are you sure she is okay?"

"The baby is perfectly fine ... heartbeat is strong and healthy," she replied.

"Thank God for that! This can't be happening to me right now. I can't go on bed rest! What am I going to do? I have everything calculated ... all of my paychecks. I will only receive six weeks' leave and still have two and a half months before I give birth." Melissa began sobbing. "How will I provide?"

Sandra said to her, "Don't worry, sweetheart. I'm sure your husband will be there to help support you. Everything will work out. The most important thing is that the baby is born healthy."

Melissa's mind began to race. *She just doesn't know how Raymond is. He's going to be so upset*, Melissa thought. The fact was Melissa had been the only one working at the moment and she was actually supporting Raymond. Raymond had been out of work, once again.

CHAPTER 2

Not Part of the Plan

Blessed is the one who perseveres under trial because, having stood the test, that person will receive the crown of life that the Lord has promised to those who love him.

—James 1:12 (NIV)

T HE SUBWAY TRAIN ride from the midwife's office, located on the Upper East Side of Manhattan, en route to work seemed to take forever. Melissa was overwhelmed with worry. She prayed, "God, how will I provide for my babies? I didn't plan on this happening? Raymond will never go for this. Please make a way for us, Lord."

When she arrived at work, she was sweating profusely because of her nerves. She gasped for air, drowning in a state of uneasiness. How was she going to tell her boss that she had to go on maternity leave two and a half months before her baby was due? She hadn't even trained anyone to do her job yet. This wasn't the plan she had in mind. Melissa's heart thumped in her chest. Her eyes were threaded with red and were puffy from all of the crying she had done the night before. Maternity leave pay was only for six weeks. Two months and change, plus her actual maternity leave, would be too much time away from work and without pay. What if they replaced her permanently?

When she walked into her boss's office, Melissa's face said it all.

"Hi, Melissa, come in. Have a seat … What's going on?" Elaine asked.

Melissa looked down. As she swallowed hard, she looked up, and before she could say the words, with her hormones rocketing sky high, she began to cry. Like perfectly pear-shaped droplets of rain that race down a windowpane, Melissa's tears just rolled off of her cheeks.

"Oh no, sweetheart! What's the matter?" her boss said, as she grabbed tissue from her desk and handed it over to her.

Melissa said, "I don't have very good news."

Elaine looked at her, waiting to hear what the bad news was.

"Oh no, sweetheart. Is the baby okay?"

Melissa continued, "My midwife has ordered me to go on bed rest. My cervix is one centimeter opened, and the baby is at risk if born prematurely. I don't know what I'm going to do. I have everything calculated, and this is just not good for me."

Melissa began crying with her face in her hands. Elaine walked around from behind her desk toward Melissa and gave her a big hug. She told her not to worry and walked back over to her chair. She picked up the phone. Elaine then called the human resources director.

"Nina, hi … Could you do me a big favor? Please let me know how many vacation and sick days Melissa has for the rest of the year. Thank you."

Elaine said, "You were very brave to make it into work today. You should have just called me from home. I am calling our company car service to have them drive you home now. Don't worry. We'll figure something out, and I will call you later or by tomorrow morning. The most important thing is that you and your baby are fine."

Melissa's coworkers all said goodbye and wished her well before leaving to go home.

Later, upon finally arriving home, she called Raymond to pick up their baby girl, Sarah, from the babysitter. The call went straight to voice mail. Melissa sensed something might have been wrong. Raymond had given his word earlier that he would pick the baby up. Melissa then called her dad.

"Dad, can you please pick up Sarah for me? Raymond's phone is off, and he was supposed to pick her up. I think something may be wrong," Melissa said. "I just don't get it. I spoke with him about an hour before I left work."

The hours crawled by and still no word from Raymond. Melissa called her mother-in-law, and she too was worried. Melissa began calling hospitals and local precincts, looking for Raymond. Meanwhile, in the South Bronx, Raymond sat in jail. Back at home, the telephone rang. Melissa immediately picked up. It was her father, David.

He said, "Melissa, I found him. I found Raymond. He's at a precinct in the South Bronx. He's been arrested. I'm on my way to pick you up. Your mother will stay with Sarah."

"Arrested? What do you mean he's been arrested?"

But he had already hung up.

On their way to the precinct, Melissa was too shocked and nervous to cry.

She said, "What in the world could he have been arrested for? I don't understand."

David said, "Don't worry, honey. We are going to find out. I'm here for you, sweetheart. This will all be sorted out."

They both finally arrived at the precinct. When they walked in, Melissa noticed the dim gray walls. She looked over to her immediate right and saw a man with makeup, sitting handcuffed. She looked to her left and saw the commotion of police officers walking in and out. She then looked to the right of the main front desk and noticed three women chained to each other. The women were clearly women of the street. As Melissa and David approached the front desk, her father asked for information on Raymond. As Melissa nervously nibbled on a saltine cracker, David asked the front desk sergeant, "Good evening, Officer. I'm here to find out about my son-in-law, Raymond Perez. What has he been arrested for?"

The officer said, "Oh yeah, Raymond Perez. He was picked up earlier this evening. Let me call the arresting officer." The front desk sergeant picked up the phone. "Yeah, Anderson, come down to the front"

The sergeant said to David, "She'll be right down."

David asked, surprised, "She? … Oh, okay. Thank you."

The arresting officer walked in. She was quite striking. The detective had black hair pulled up in a neat ponytail, a sun-kissed complexion, and a lean build. She was wearing blue jeans and a black sweatshirt.

The detective introduced herself. "Hi, I'm Detective Anderson. How can I help you?" she said as she shook David's hand.

David said, "Oh … hello, Detective Anderson. I'm David Rodriguez. So were you the one who arrested my son-in-law, Raymond Perez?"

She said, "Yes, I am."

"Why was he arrested?"

"I'm so sorry, sir, but he asked me not to divulge that information. You're going to have to ask him that yourself. All

I can tell you is that he was picked up on a sweep earlier this evening. I'm sorry, sir."

As the detective looked over at a panic-stricken Melissa, she shook her head empathetically.

David's face became as white as a ghost.

Melissa asked David, "What's wrong, Dad?"

He said loudly, "That good for nothing! I hope it's not what I'm thinking."

Melissa's father was a retired police officer himself, so he understood the cop lingo and terminology.

"What happened, Dad? Who's good for nothing?"

"Love, I'm talking about Raymond. I'm sorry, but I just hope it's not what I'm thinking," David said angrily.

"What are you thinking? Dad, please talk to me!" Melissa nervously demanded.

"Sweetheart, let's just go home. We can't do anything right now. He's going before a judge tomorrow morning."

Then David turned his attention back to the detective. He said, "Thank you for your time, Detective Anderson."

CHAPTER 3

Red Flags

But he said to me, "My grace is sufficient for you, for my power is made perfect in weakness." Therefore I will boast all the more gladly about my weaknesses, so that Christ's power may rest on me. That is why, for Christ's sake, I delight in weaknesses, in insults, in hardships, in persecutions, in difficulties. For when I am weak, then I am strong.
—2 Corinthians 12:9–10 (NIV)

IN THE CAR, on the way back home from the precinct with her father, Melissa wondered why all of this had happened. She began to feel as if everything was her fault. Feelings of guilt weighed heavily on her. She began to think back to all of the signs that indicated trouble from the very beginning of her relationship with Raymond.

Almost Three Years Earlier

After a long, hard day at work, Melissa and a coworker decided to unwind and grab a bite to eat. Every Wednesday was karaoke night at The Melody Café in Midtown Manhattan. Melissa and

Liza particularly loved to sing the popular song "I Will Survive" on karaoke nights after a long, stressful day at work. They were both intelligent, single, beautiful, and quickly climbing up the corporate ladder. Liza was a belt designer, while Melissa was assistant designer of handbags for a huge accessories company in Midtown Manhattan. After eating their buffalo chicken wings, they decided to burn off some steam on the dance floor. Across the room were a few obnoxious, loud young men, trying to grab the ladies' attention. Melissa and Liza continued on dancing and having fun. Here came one of the young men, wearing a gray polo shirt and black slacks. He was about five-eleven with dark, slicked-back hair. He was attractive with olive skin and hazel eyes. The young man had noticed Melissa from across the room and wondered who this stunningly beautiful brunette was. She had long, beautiful, thick dark-brown hair, which hung down to the middle of her back. She wore a red pencil skirt and a black blouse with three-and-a-half-inch open-toe patent-leather black heels. She had almond-shaped chestnut-brown eyes and flawless porcelain skin.

"Hi, can I borrow your friend here?" the gentleman asked Liza.

Melissa quickly responded, "No, thank you. I'm dancing with my friend."

"Ahh, c'mon. I'm a pretty good dancer. I promise I won't bite."

Liza said, "All right. Well, you'll have to dance with the both of us. My friend here is kinda shy."

Melissa nodded her head before the guy could take notice and let out a quick sigh of annoyance.

Liza leaned in on Melissa and whispered into her ear, "C'mon, lighten up. He is kinda cute."

After the song was over, as they got ready to walk off the

dance floor, the gentleman gently grabbed Melissa's hand. "Hey, what's your name?"

"I'm Melissa, and this is my friend, Liza. What's your name?"

"I'm Raymond."

One Year after Meeting Each Other

"We've been together for almost a year, and you haven't decided if you want to get married?" Raymond said, frustrated.

"I think we need some more time, Raymond," Melissa replied.

"More time for what? You're going to be *thirty* soon, and I'm *thirty-five*. I love you. I thought you loved me too?" Raymond asked.

"I do, but—"

"But? But what? Don't you see a good thing when it's in front of you? Let's see how you'll do without me! You won't find a better man than me," Raymond said angrily.

"Excuse me? Raymond, I think you should leave. I don't like the way you're speaking to me," Melissa said.

"Oh ... I'm sorry, mama ... C'mon. You know I just love you. That's all," Raymond said.

"I think you need to go. Call me later. I just need some space right now. Please."

"I'm sorry, love. You are the best thing that ever happened to me. I'm sorry I flew off the handle like that. I'll give you space. I just don't want to lose you. I'll call you later," Raymond said as he leaned over to hug her, but Melissa discreetly shrugged him away from her.

Six Months Later

It was only a couple of weeks before Melissa and Raymond's wedding. They were getting married at their church, Disciples of Christ. Melissa was consumed with doubts and felt guilty about how she was feeling. So she decided to meet with the senior pastor of their church for counseling and advice.

"Good morning Pastor Delgado. Thank you so much for meeting with me this morning."

Pastor Delgado said, "Of course, Melissa, it is always my pleasure. How can I help you, dear?"

"Pastor, I've been feeling doubtful and guilty lately."

"About what?"

"Well … it's Raymond. As you know, we are getting married in only two weeks, and I think I may be making a mistake. I do love him, but I just feel maybe it's not the right time."

"Melissa, it's perfectly normal for some people to get cold feet before making this very important commitment to each other. Have you had this conversation with Raymond?" Pastor Delgado counseled.

"Yes, I have, Pastor … Well, kind of. But he's very insistent and tells me that we are not getting any younger. Pastor Delgado, do you remember the sermon that you preached just a few weeks ago on how God always shows us red flags? And how He's always guiding us in the way we should go?"

Pastor Delgado answered, "Yes, Melissa. But remember that even when we ignore the warnings and we make wrong decisions, the Lord always finds a way to reroute us. No matter what, He's always with us. Melissa, are you saying that there are red flags in your relationship with Raymond?"

"Yes, Pastor, I am. There are a quite few of them, and I'm actually kinda scared."

"Oh dear, I'm sorry. Tell me what's going on? What are you scared of? I'm sorry to ask this, but is Raymond hurting you in any way?"

"No, no, no … Pastor. This was probably a mistake coming here. I guess it's just cold feet, like you said."

"Wait a minute. Hold on. I think maybe I could call Raymond and arrange for a couple's meeting with both of you."

"No! No! That won't be necessary. Please don't call Raymond. He has no idea I'm here meeting with you today, and I don't want to hurt him. I'm so sorry to have wasted your time today, Pastor Delgado. I'll be fine." Melissa quickly looked down at her watch. She said, "Oh wow, I'm so sorry. I have to be somewhere. Thank you so much! I'll be fine, Pastor. I'll see you at service on Sunday." She quickly scurried out of his office.

Pastor Delgado said, "Wait! Melissa! Don't forget about our couples' retreat day this Saturday."

"Yeah, sure. I'm sorry, Pastor. I gotta run … thanks!"

Pastor Delgado sat down in his chair with a look of confusion and concern.

"Melissa, sweetheart, we're here." David gently patted Melissa. Melissa opened her eyes and was brought back to her present reality. She looked over at David while they still sat in the car and said, "I feel so guilty for saying this, but all of the signs were there, and I ignored every single one."

"What are you talking about, sweetheart?" David said.

"Pastor Delgado once preached a sermon about how God always directs our steps. He said how God shows you the signs for which way to go and the red flags as warnings of which way not to go. I saw so many red flags when I met Raymond. Aww, Dad, am I a bad person for even bringing this up? He's my husband now, and I made a vow for better or for worse. And I have beautiful Sarah, who I couldn't ever imagine my life without," Melissa sadly said.

"Melissa, you're a wonderful woman. Don't feel guilty. Raymond is a grown man. What happened to him today is completely his own doing. He's responsible for his own actions.

I wish you would talk with me more. I never knew that you had reservations about him from the beginning."

"What are you talking about, Dad? Even you didn't like him for me," Melissa said.

"Sweetheart, I didn't outright say that I didn't like him for you. I merely told you that I felt you two were rushing into things and to give yourselves time. I just knew that things haven't been right between you two lately," David said. "I just couldn't put my finger on it. Mel, Raymond is good to you, right?"

Melissa froze at his question.

"Mel?" David asked.

"Uh, yeah, Dad, of course. I have a lot going on right now. I'm sorry, I know I brought it up, but do you mind if we stop talking about how things are between me and Raymond? I just want this night to be over," Melissa said.

"Of course, sweetheart," David replied. "We can talk about this another time."

CHAPTER 4

A Deal with the Devil

Be alert and of sober mind. Your enemy the devil prowls around like
a roaring lion looking for someone to devour. Resist him, standing
firm in the faith, because you know that the family of believers
throughout the world is undergoing the same kind of sufferings. And
the God of all grace, who called you to his eternal glory in Christ, after
you have suffered for a little while, will himself restore you and make
you strong, firm and steadfast. To him be the power for ever and ever.
Amen.

—1 Peter 5:8–11 (NIV)

Presently

THE NIGHT SKY was clear. The air was crisp and cold.
Melissa quickly changed the subject back to the problem at
hand.

"I don't understand why Raymond was arrested!" she cried.
"Why do you think the officer wouldn't tell you the charges?"

"Sweetheart, I'm so sorry. You don't need this kind of stress.
It's not good for you and the baby," said David. "We don't have

to talk about this right now. And I don't want you home alone with Sarah either. Why don't you both stay with me and your mother tonight?"

"Aww, Dad, we'll be okay."

"No, no. You're staying with us tonight. I don't want you home alone. Besides, tomorrow is Christmas Eve, and your mom could use your help preparing Christmas Eve supper. What do you think?"

"Aw, all right," Melissa sadly said.

"Come on, love. You need some rest. Go upstairs and grab a few items of clothing for you and Sarah. I'll wait down here for you, since there is no parking."

"All right, Dad, thank you for being so good to us. I love you so much," Melissa said as she hugged her father.

Meanwhile Back at the Precinct

While Raymond sat in the jail cell, he heard two sets of footsteps down the corridor. One of the detectives walked with another gentleman, a very well-dressed man. Raymond mumbled small words of gratitude, "Finally … a lawyer." But he noticed the man's hands were not visible.

The detective opened the gate as Raymond glanced down toward his feet, and he placed the sharply dressed man in the cell with him. Raymond looked up at the gentleman, kind of confused. He asked, "Are you an attorney?"

The sharply dressed man laughed and answered, "Nah, man, I've been arrested … I'm in the pharmaceutical business. I've been wrongly arrested. But my attorney will have me outta here soon, and you? Why are you here?"

Raymond answered, "Um, well … it's all a misunderstanding. Let's just say, I was at the wrong place at the wrong time."

"Well, what do they have you in for?" the man asked.

"Well … they're saying I was trying to hook up with a call girl."

"Ahh, that's it? Don't worry. This is just a slap on the wrist. You'll be outta here by tomorrow."

"How do you know?" Raymond asked.

"Listen, what you committed is a class B misdemeanor. Most of the time, the judge will probably just make you pay a penalty fee or give you some kind of community service if you have no priors," the man explained.

"My family can never find out about this," said Raymond.

"Are you married?"

"Yes," Raymond replied.

"Kids?"

"Yes," Raymond responded in a low voice. "I have a one-year-old daughter, and my wife is pregnant with our second baby."

"Mmm, sounds complicated. Too bad for you." The man laughed. "I'm just kidding, bro. What line of work are you in?" the man asked.

"Well, I'm kind of between jobs right now," Raymond said.

"Really? So, in other words, you don't have a job. 'Cause I'm currently looking for someone to assist me with my pharmaceutical business. And I also run a dating service. Would you be interested?"

"Dating service? How does that work?" Raymond asked.

"Well, I run the service exclusively for men who are looking for a date or just want to have company. Ain't nothin' wrong with hiring a girl for company, right?" the man said as he winked at Raymond.

"Ahhh, okay, right … dating service … I get it. Where is your business located?"

The man thought for a second and then said, "It's located

downtown, near Alphabet City. But I provide services for all five boroughs here in New York."

"Oh wow!" exclaimed Raymond. "Sounds cool! Yeah, I guess I am interested."

"I'm also in the process of creating an online setup to expand the business," the man said. "By the way, I'm Mike … and you are?"

"I'm Raymond, Raymond Perez."

"Is your wife going to be okay with that? 'Cause I need somebody reliable. And if need be, I need you available for seven days a week. Besides, what possessed you to get married anyway? Ain't no way I'm gonna answer to any chick out here."

"Seven days a week?" Raymond nervously asked.

"Don't worry, Ray. I'm very flexible," Mike said. "Besides, along come some fringe benefits working for a service like this, if you know what I mean," Mike said with a smirk.

"Well, all right, sounds good to me. My wife doesn't have to know what I do. I'll just tell her I got a job at a pharmaceutical company. She doesn't have to know about the service. And I don't answer to her anyway; she answers to me."

"I like you, Ray," Mike said. "I think you're gonna be a great addition to my business."

"Wait. Where can I reach you?" Raymond asked.

"Ah, right. When you're outta here, call me after Christmas. Just look me up, 'Mike's Pharmacy,' down by the Bowery."

"Sounds good, Mike. I'm looking forward to it. Ain't this something? I met you at just the right time. Not exactly where I would expect to have a job interview though." Raymond chuckled. "But just in the nick of time."

"You're gonna make some real cash with me, Ray. You just wait and see," Mike said.

"Well, I can't wait. Now I don't have to listen to my nagging wife about getting steady work."

"Yeah, I hear you, man. That's why I ain't married. Marriage is overrated."

"What about kids? Do you have any?" Raymond asked.

"Yeah, I have one son, but his mama keeps him away from me. They live in Massachusetts. I get to see him every now and again," Mike said. "I hate to say it, but my son came to be from a one-night stand. Whatcha gonna do? Don't get me wrong; I love him and all."

"But?" Raymond asked.

"But it ain't right bringing kids into this world like that. Ahhh, I don't wanna talk about this no more."

"Well, talking about making real cash with you, will I be able to afford a suit like the one you're wearing now? What are you wearing anyway? Gucci?" asked Raymond.

"Bro, you got a good eye. I wear nothing but the best. You straight, it's Gucci."

"Shoes too?" Raymond asked.

"Straight up all Gucci, my man," Mike proudly responded. "The best part of this is I answer to no one. I'm my own boss and a self-made man. I'm gonna teach you a few tricks of the trade, Ray."

"Well, I believe everything happens for a reason," Raymond said. "I believe it's no coincidence that I met you under these circumstances. You're really saving me, bro. I can't wait to work with you."

CHAPTER 5

Punching Bag

But those who suffer he delivers in their suffering; he speaks to them in their affliction.

—Job 36:15 (NIV)

MELISSA WAS FILLED with panic. Tonight was going to be a long night for her. One quick thought came to her mind. Ironically, it was a thought that actually gave her comfort, but at the same time, it also brought on immense guilt for even thinking it. It was a quick notion that maybe Raymond had committed some serious crime that would actually put him away for a very long time. That would also mean she would finally be safe and free from him. She wouldn't have to live in fear anymore. Maybe this was a blessing in disguise. Then she closed her eyes and had a vivid memory from the past come to mind.

Raymond had used excessive force on Melissa by punching her again and again. She didn't know what hit her. The sounds of her pain echoed in the air. The white wall was a canvas of hand-painted smears of hurt.

Melissa was laid out on the floor, crying, "I'm sorry! I'm sorry!"

Melissa's eye swelled, and her lashes were heavy with tears. Her lip began to inflate right before Raymond's eyes. Then he realized they were injuries he had inflicted upon her. It was unbelievable how the bare knuckles of a man could cause such damage to another human being. Melissa had been raised in a household where her dad always honored her mother. She was taught that a man should never lay his hands on a woman. Melissa's skin was cut open. It was hard to tell exactly where her injuries were. In addition to her flesh wounds, she felt a pain inside of her heart that was an even bigger open wound. She just lay there on the floor, weeping and shivering. The floor spun in Melissa's mind. She had little to no strength left. Raymond heard Melissa's cry very faintly as his sight became blurred. Raymond was panting as if he had been running. It happened all too fast. Confused thoughts raced through his mind. What had he just done? He reached down toward Melissa. She screamed with her arms up in the air above her head, "No! Please! I'm sorry!"

Raymond said, "I'm sorry. I'm not going to hurt you again. I'm just trying to help you up."

"*Noo*! Please!" Melissa screamed again. With her arms over her head, she lay on the floor in fetal position. "Don't touch me."

"C'mon. Let me help you. I think I should take you to a hospital. Your face is hurt!"

Suddenly, there was a hard knock at the door. "Are you okay in there?" a voice asked. "Hello, Melissa? Are you okay?"

It now occurred to Raymond that it was the next-door neighbor. "Yes, she's fine," he said loudly and quickly.

The neighbor then said, "I called the police. She doesn't sound okay."

Raymond placed Melissa's arm around the back of his neck

and then proceeded to pick her up. Melissa continued to tremble uncontrollably.

"Please, just leave me alone," Melissa whimpered.

A few minutes later, there was loud banging on the door. "Open up! It's the police!"

Raymond rushed Melissa over into their bedroom. He walked toward the door, straightened out his shirt, and ran his hands through his hair to comb through it. He opened the door.

"Hi, Officer. Can I help you?"

"Ah, yes. We received a domestic call. Is your wife home?"

"Yes, she's resting inside."

The hardwood floors straightaway made a slight creaking sound. Raymond looked behind him, and it was Melissa, just standing there. The police officer took a peek inside and saw the awful mess on Melissa's face.

"Move out of the way! This woman is badly hurt!" said the officer.

"Officer, I can explain; it was an accident," Raymond said.

"Miss, what happened?" the officer asked.

But Melissa kept trembling while she looked at Raymond. She would not respond.

"We need to get her to a hospital right away," said the officer. "Why didn't you call an ambulance?" the officer asked Raymond.

"Umm, she said she was fine."

"Well, what happened? How did this happen to her?" the officer asked.

"She just fell," Raymond said while gawking at Melissa. "Right, honey?"

Melissa just nodded as she stared down at the floor.

The officer radioed in for an ambulance. Upon arrival at the hospital, Melissa was immediately rushed into the emergency room area. A triage nurse began asking her a lot of questions.

She then asked, "Ma'am, are you afraid of anyone at home?"

Melissa just had a blank look on her face.

"Ma'am? Did you understand the question?" the nurse asked.

Melissa just continued to sit silently.

"Did someone do this to you?"

But she refused to respond.

"Okay. A doctor will be right in to see you. We are here to help. Please do not be afraid to talk with us."

But she just lay there, expressionless. Within a few minutes, a doctor walked in.

"Hi, I'm Dr. Anagnos. Melissa, right?" he said as he looked at the paperwork on his clipboard.

Melissa just nodded.

"Okay, Melissa, can you tell me what happened?" the doctor asked as he examined her face. "It appears that you have a laceration just above your cheek here … and one on the right side of your forehead. These are pretty bad."

Melissa started welling up with tears, and they slowly rolled down her face—but still, not a word out of her.

"Do you want to tell me what happened? I can't help you if you don't communicate with me. Did someone do this to you? I want to help you."

Melissa looked over at the curtain and quickly noticed a set of black military-style shoes she recognized. It was the police officer who had escorted her to the hospital. She suspected that he might be listening in.

Suddenly, she said loudly, "I fell. I … was in the kitchen and tripped and hit my head against the table; that's all."

The words trembled out of Melissa's mouth as she explained to the doctor what had happened. But the doctor gave her a look of suspicion.

He replied, "Dear, how then did you get lacerations on two different areas of your face? Did you trip and fall?"

"Yes," Melissa replied.

"Your explanation just doesn't add up with your injuries. You are safe here. Tell me what really happened."

Melissa started to weep uncontrollably. "I told you what happened. Please. I just want to be left alone."

"Well, you're going to need sutures. And I'm going to have a CAT scan and some x-rays done. I'd like to do blood work as well."

"I'm fine. I just want to go home."

"You are not fine. We need to close up your wounds. And I need to make sure all is okay internally with you."

"How soon do you think I'll be outta here?" Melissa desperately asked.

"As soon as we get all of your tests done," the doctor replied. "Is anyone here with you?"

Melissa reluctantly replied, "Ah yes, my ... my husband."

"I'd like to speak with him," the doctor said. "What is his name?"

"Raymond," said Melissa.

Melissa also pleaded with the officer, "Officer, I already told you that I fell. Please. I'd like to just go home."

"Mrs. Perez, just sit back and relax. Everything is going to be okay."

But she thought quite the opposite. It wasn't going to be okay. It hadn't been okay for a long time. But she also believed that it was only the grace of God that had kept her somewhat sane throughout this tsunami of problems she continued to face in her new marriage.

The doctor stepped out into the waiting area, looking for

Raymond. He saw a man sitting on a chair with his head leaned over, bent down with his hands on his head.

The doctor said, "Mr. Perez?"

Raymond jolted up out of his chair.

"Uh, yeah, how is she, Doc?" Raymond shook his hand.

"She's doing fine for now. I'm a little concerned about your wife, Mr. Perez. She's not telling me what really happened."

"Well, what did she say?" Raymond asked curiously.

"Mr. Perez, what happened to your wife?"

"It was an accident, Doc."

"How was it an accident?"

"Am I allowed to see her now? I really need to see my wife."

"Mr. Perez, you'll be allowed to see her as soon as you communicate with me. I am only trying to help her."

"I'm sorry, Doc. I need to see her." Raymond walked away.

Standing outside of Melissa's room was the police officer who had escorted her to the hospital.

"You can't go in there," the officer said to Raymond.

"Why not? I want to see my wife."

"I am waiting to ask her a couple more questions," the officer replied.

"She doesn't have to talk to you. Besides, she already told you that nothing happened. So unless you're going to charge us with anything, I think we are done here."

Then another voice chimed in. "Mr. Perez, I'm sorry but your wife is being sutured up right now. She also seems to be distressed. It's best if you wait here for the doctor to speak with you," a nurse said.

"Okay, but I'm waiting right here," said Raymond in a resentful tone.

Inside of the room, while the physician's assistant was suturing up Melissa's wounds, she began talking with her.

"How are you feeling? Please let me know if I'm hurting you," the PA said.

"I'm fine. Thank you. I just want to go home," Melissa said.

"Are you here with anyone?"

"Yes," Melissa said. "My husband is right outside waiting."

"Oh, that's good. What about your kids?"

"Aw, no, we don't have any kids yet. In fact, we've only been married for three months," Melissa responded somberly.

"Oh, wow, newlyweds! Well, congratulations," the PA said.

But Melissa didn't respond.

The PA then asked, "How did this happen to you?"

"I fell," Melissa quickly responded.

"How did you fall? It must've been a bad fall." Even as the PA commented, she had a look of uncertainty as to Melissa's response.

"I'm sorry; I'm just really tired right now. I don't want to talk about it anymore," Melissa said.

"Aww, honey. I've been doing this for a while. Working in this ER, you see a lot of things you don't want to see sometimes. I don't want to pry but just want to tell you that you're not alone. There are many resources to get help with whatever it is you're going through," she said. "It's not easy to believe that these wounds are the result of a simple fall. By the way, my name is Mary."

"Thanks, Mary. I appreciate your concern. But I already told everyone what happened," Melissa said.

Melissa noticed a cross around Mary's neck. She asked, "Are you a Christian?"

"Yes, honey. I am. And you?"

"Yes, I am too," Melissa said.

"Sweetheart, since we are on the topic, whatever it is that you're going through, just pray. Pray to Him for guidance and direction. He always shows us the way. And I am going to pray for you too, love. I don't usually do this, but here's my number if you ever need a friend to talk to," said the PA as she jotted it down on a piece of paper.

"Thank you so much, Mary. For some reason, I do feel a little bit better after talking with you. It's not often that I meet people who talk to me about God. I am also a big believer in the power of prayer. Thank you," Melissa said as tears rolled down her face.

The curtain suddenly opened. It was Dr. Anagnos.

"Melissa, we just got the result of your urine sample. And I'm happy to tell you that you're pregnant!"

"What!" Melissa exclaimed.

"Yes, your test came back positive. I am going to do a sonogram just to see how the baby looks," the doctor explained.

"Baby? How can that be? Are you sure?" Melissa asked.

Melissa didn't know how to feel. This was a dream come true, an answered prayer. She had always wanted children and had prayed for this moment. But the circumstances she had been under were quite far from normal, and she wasn't particularly expecting to hear that right then. She sat there with a black eye, two large cuts on her face, and dried mascara streaks down her face. Immediately, she prayed in her mind.

"We won't be able to take x-rays, but we'll do routine blood work," her doctor said.

"Can I please speak to my husband?" Melissa asked.

Mary was then done with suturing up Melissa. She said, "I'll go and get him. What's his name?"

"It's Raymond," said Melissa.

Mary stepped out and saw a man standing right outside of where Melissa was. He looked disheveled. She asked, "Are you Raymond?"

"Yes," Raymond replied.

"Hi, your wife is asking for ya," Mary said.

Raymond immediately walked in and saw Melissa. "Aw, man … you look terrible. I'm so sorry."

He hugged Melissa tight, but Melissa didn't hug him back; her arms remained by her side.

"How are you feeling?" Raymond asked.

"I don't know yet. But I have to tell you something," Melissa replied.

"What?"

"I'm … I'm pregnant."

"Pregnant!" Raymond exclaimed. "Baby, that's great news."

But Melissa didn't share the same excitement, not because of the baby, but because she feared Raymond. She ached not only physically but emotionally too.

"Baby, I'm so sorry. You will never have to go through this again. I lost my temper. Please forgive me. I promise I won't ever hurt you again."

But Melissa didn't believe him. Any ideas that Melissa contemplated about leaving Raymond after this suddenly were put on hold. She was raised to make a marriage work, and terminating a pregnancy was also not an option under any circumstance for her. Deep down inside, she was grateful about a new baby, but Melissa felt stuck. How did she wind up this way? She had always considered herself to be a strong, confident woman. She also knew babies were a gift from the Lord. Maybe things were going to change for the better. Maybe fatherhood would reform Raymond and renew him. Maybe Raymond really did mean it this time, that he would never hurt her again. Only time would tell. Melissa was also taught to forgive easily. This was quite difficult for her, but she forgave Raymond in her heart. Despite the emotional and verbal abuse, he had never physically hurt her before that night. She hoped this would be the first and the last time that this happened.

Melissa awoke from her nightmare, only to realize the nightmare was real. Right then, she lay there thinking she had entered into another trial. She was anxious to find out what had happened to Raymond this time.

CHAPTER 6

No Place Like Home

> Anyone who does not provide for their relatives, and especially for their own household, has denied the faith and is worse than an unbeliever.
>
> —1 Timothy 5:8 (NIV)

Christmas Eve Morning

THERE SHE WENT, with short baby breaths and quick pauses for recovery breaks in between; baby Sarah continued to cry. Melissa awoke to her baby's cries. She walked over, picked little Sarah up, and soothed her.

"Hi, baby, what's the matter? Waaas da matta, huh?" Melissa said in a gibberish, baby-like voice.

Baby Sarah laid her head on Melissa's chest. She sat on the bed and began breast-feeding her.

"Thank You, Lord, for another day. Thank You for this beautiful little gift You've blessed me with. Lord, please console me. I don't understand what's going on with Raymond, but our family really needs You now," Melissa prayed under her breath.

The door suddenly opened.

"How are my two girls doing?" Maria asked.

"Good morning, Ma," Melissa replied. "We're good. Aren't we, Sarah?" Melissa smiled down at her baby. "Ma, as soon as I'm done feeding Sarah, I'll help you start preparing dinner for later."

"Don't you worry yourself, sweetheart. Last night, I already prepared the potato salad and stuffing. I also seasoned the roast last night, and in fact, I already popped it into the oven. If you want, you can help with the rice and garden salad," said Maria.

"Okay, Ma."

"I'm going to run out to the market to buy a few more things that we need for later. Do you need anything?"

"No, I don't need anything, thanks," Melissa replied.

"All right, love, I'll see you in a bit."

After she fed and changed little Sarah, she placed her in the playpen. Upon entering the living room of her parents' apartment, she looked at their beautifully decorated gold, white, and green Christmas tree. The couch was a rich off-white crème color with garnet-red throw pillows on it. The burning peppermint-candy-cane-scented candle sat on the cherrywood coffee table, and she smelled the aroma of coffee and pancakes lingering from the kitchen.

"Good morning, sweetheart!" said David. "How did you sleep?"

"Not great, Daddy, but I'm okay."

"I made your favorite—chocolate-chip pancakes," David said.

"You're the best! I'm not really hungry, but I'll have just one. Thank you, Daddy."

"Any word from Raymond yet?" asked David.

"Nope, not yet. Ugh, I have agita," said Melissa. "Dad, now that Ma isn't here. What did you mean last night when you said that you hope it's not what you're thinking? I'm a grown woman, Dad. I can handle it."

"Uh, sweetheart, it's complicated. I don't want you to be stressed out."

"Please talk to me, Daddy."

"Well, this is going to be really hard for me to say out loud. But as a cop, I remember times when we'd arrest someone for solicitation. I just can't understand why Raymond would ask the detective not to tell us the real reason for his arrest. It's suspicious. Either that or he was caught with drugs. But we don't know him to do that kind of stuff, and he's not really a drinker either."

"Solicitation? Daddy! Are you saying Raymond was looking for a call girl?" Melissa asked in a disturbed tone. "How could you say that? I can't even fathom that idea. He wouldn't do that!"

"This is why I didn't want to tell you. I'm going to have a long talk with him as soon as he's out," David said.

"Dad, no, please! I'll just talk to him," Melissa said. "I know you mean well, Dad, but this is my problem. I can handle it."

"No, no. I've been sensing for a long time that something hasn't been right between the two of you," David replied.

"There you go again, Daddy, please. I can take care of myself."

"I just worry about you. Most important, I worry about Sarah and my other grandbaby you're carrying."

"Don't worry about us, Dad. I promise you that if I need your or Mom's help, I will ask," Melissa said.

"It just gets me so upset. Raymond is not working. And now, he got arrested. Sweetheart, you're a great wife, and Raymond needs to be a good, providing husband," David said.

"Dad! Stop. He's trying. I told you we are fine. Besides, I make a pretty good living," Melissa replied.

"What about your early maternity leave? Are you two going to be able to manage?" David asked worriedly.

"Yes. Dad, give me a minute. I just want to check on Sarah." Melissa walked away to avoid any more pressing questions.

Melissa began sweating; her heart had stomped in her chest, and she became slightly faint as her anxiety got the best of her.

"Oh no! Daa—" Melissa yelled out as she fell to the ground.

David heard a loud thump in the bedroom.

"Melissa!" David ran in to see Melissa passed out on the floor.

"Melissa! Honey, wake up!" David quickly ran out of the bedroom toward the bathroom to run cold water over a hand towel. He quickly returned to Melissa and placed the cold towel on her head.

"Sweetheart! Wake up!"

Sarah started crying. Suddenly, there were babbling noises ...

"*Mmmammammammama,*" Sarah babbled loudly in her playpen.

"Sarah! You said, 'Mama'!" David exclaimed. "Oh my goodness, you just said, 'Mama'!"

Melissa suddenly opened her eyes.

"Dad, where's Sarah?"

"Honey, she's right here. Are you okay?"

"Yeah, I guess ... Did I just pass out again?"

"Yes, sweetheart. How's your head? I need to take you to the hospital."

"No, Dad! I'm fine. It's just low blood sugar. I'm fine."

"Sweetheart, Sarah called out for you," David said excitedly. "She called out for 'Mama.'"

"She what?" Melissa asked, confused.

"Sarah said, 'Mama.'"

Melissa carefully sat up while still on the floor.

"Baby! Did you say, 'Mama'?" Melissa began to cry. She was crying uncontrollably. But they didn't appear to be tears of joy.

"Whoa, whoa, sweetheart. What's the matter?" David said as he hugged her.

"I can't take the stress. Raymond is locked up, it's Christmas Eve, I just fainted, and we both missed our baby's first and most important word, *mama*. This is all too much for me, Daddy. I'm tired of being strong." Melissa continued to sob. "Not to mention, I'm extra hormonal, which doesn't help."

David looked at Melissa and said, "Come on; hold my hand."

Melissa grabbed her father's hand.

"I'm going to pray. Lord, we want to thank You for this day. We thank You for the grace that You give us daily to handle anything that comes our way. We thank You that no weapon formed against our family will prosper. Lord, please help my daughter. Give her peace. Lord, as difficult as it is right now, we will be still and know that You are God. Please bring my son-in-law home soon. We need You. Melissa and Sarah need You. Thank You for not allowing us to be discouraged or scared during this time. We trust Your will in our family life. In Jesus's name, we pray. Amen."

"Amen! Thank you, Daddy," Melissa said and then wrapped her arms around her father.

CHAPTER 7

A Fresh Start

Create in me a pure heart, O God, and renew a steadfast spirit within
me. Do not cast me from your presence or take your Holy Spirit from
me. Restore to me the joy of your salvation and grant me a willing
spirit, to sustain me.

—Psalm 51:10–12 (NIV)

Christmas Eve Afternoon

THE CLEAR BLUE skies were scattered with a few white
cotton-like clouds. The door swiftly swung open from the
east side of the criminal courthouse in the Bronx. As Raymond
walked out of the courthouse, he wondered how he had wound
up there in the first place. But it was just as Mike had explained
to him; he had gotten off easy, just a slap on the wrist. The judge
let him out on an ROR—released on his own recognizance.
He was ordered to pay a four-hundred-dollar penalty fee and
promised not to engage in any illegal activity while out on his

ROR. Raymond thought this was a piece of cake. Not to mention, he had walked out of jail with a new job opportunity.

That seemed too good to be true for him. His family was the last thing on his mind at the moment. He had been thinking about the money he was going to make soon. The street bustled with cars. He looked over to his left and observed an older couple. The woman was wearing an ivory suit and holding a small white bouquet of hydrangeas, and the man with her was wearing a dark navy-blue suit and zoot-suit-like hat. They looked so happy and were obviously newly married. Raymond hadn't seen Melissa smile the way that woman was smiling in a very long time.

"Thanks for coming, Mami," said Raymond. "Thanks for paying my fine too. I promise I'll pay you back."

"What in the world is wrong with you?" exclaimed Raymond's mother. "Does Melissa know about any of this?"

"Nah, David brought her to the precinct last night, but the cops didn't tell them. Don't worry; I got this," Raymond confidently said. "I gotta hurry home. Thanks for bringing my car. I'll drop you off first." He quickly gave her a peck on the cheek.

"What are you going to tell her?" Raymond's mother asked worriedly. "I'm so embarrassed and have not answered any of her calls. I don't want to be a part of your shenanigans or lies."

"Stop, Mami. I told you not to worry about it. I'll handle it," Raymond said.

"I'm not going to stop, Raymond! You think that you're invincible. Your unsavory actions are going to catch up with you one day, and I want no part of it. I'm sorry to say this, Son, but you're going to put me in my grave early," Raymond's mom said. "Since you were a kid, you've always given me a hard time; you're just like your father."

"Yeah! A father that I never met! So please, stop it with that!

I don't want to hear it anymore!" Raymond shouted. "Enough of this! I gotta get home."

An Hour after Raymond's Release from Jail

The doorbell rang.

Maria said, "Mel, can you see who's at the door?"

"Sure, Mom," Melissa replied. She looked through the peephole and let out a loud yell, "Raymond!" She opened the door, and Raymond immediately grabbed a tight hold of her and hugged her with his head buried in her shoulder.

"Melissa, I'm so sorry," Raymond said.

"Raymond! What happened? Why were you arrested?"

"Ah, these cops are ridiculous. I was charged with disorderly conduct," Raymond explained.

"Disorderly conduct? For what?" Melissa asked.

"It's a long story, Mel."

"*Well*? I got all of the time in the world. Please do tell," Melissa said.

"I've been stressed out not having any work. I had a little too much to drink and—"

Melissa interrupted, "Too much to drink? But you don't really drink."

"I know … Well, that's just it. I had a couple of drinks because of all of the stress lately. I guess I was driving past the speed limit. Got stopped, and I was a little out of line with the officer. That's it."

"Are you serious?" Melissa asked. "So how did you get out?"

"Nothing serious. The judge ordered me to pay a fine. That was it," explained Raymond. "I just want to put this behind me. Besides, it's Christmas, and we're all together. That's all that matters, right?"

"Yeah, I guess," Melissa said with doubt in her tone.

David overheard his lame explanation for his arrest, but he had a keen intuition; he knew better. He didn't want to approach Raymond about it in depth in front of Melissa because of her earlier stress and being pregnant. David was livid, but that day, it didn't seem like the right time.

"Raymond," called David.

"Hey, Dave," said Raymond. "Thanks for taking care of my girls." He looked over at little Sarah and Melissa.

"Well, Raymond, they're my girls too, so no need to thank me," said David. "Let me ask you a question … Why wouldn't the detective tell me what you were arrested for?"

"Dave, I don't know," Raymond said while he shrugged his shoulders.

"Oh, but you do know!" David said loudly. "The officer was very clear in telling me that *you* did not want her telling us!"

"You know how these cops are; they're a bunch of liars," Raymond said confidently.

"Ray, you forget, I'm a retired police officer. I took my job very seriously and always worked with integrity. So I don't take too kindly to demeaning opinions toward police officers."

"Sorry, Pops, you know how I feel toward cops these days. Nothing personal, but you definitely are the exception," Raymond said.

"So let me ask you this: You were drinking a little too much? Did they give you a breathalyzer?"

"Um, yeah. They did," Raymond rolled his eyes.

"And? You didn't mention anything about DWI? What happened to your license?" asked David.

"Pops, I'm good. I wasn't drunk. I got nasty with the officer and resisted his orders to move my car. That's all. Listen, it's Christmas. Do we have to talk about this now?"

"Well, we will talk about this, but I guess now isn't the right time. None of what you said makes any sense to me. But Melissa doesn't need any more stress," David said. "But you and I are definitely going to talk."

"Dad, please. The important thing is that we are all together," Melissa said. "Is your mom coming later?"

Raymond responded, "Nah, she's not feeling well. Said she couldn't sleep last night. I know it's my fault."

"I tried calling her a few times but got no answer. I also know she was worried sick about you too," Melissa said.

"We'll figure out something. Maybe we'll go visit her in a couple days when she's better," Raymond said.

"Ray, please promise me that we never have to go through this again?" Melissa pleaded.

"I promise we won't. This will never happen again," Raymond said. "Consider this a fresh start for us. I also never had the chance to tell you that I got a job."

"A new job? That's great news, Ray! Where?"

"At a pharmaceutical company in Manhattan doing sales," he said.

"Oh my goodness! This is so good!" Melissa hugged him. "I was so worried with having to stop work. I was worried about money. I didn't really want to touch my savings if I didn't have to. I really want to believe that it will be a fresh start."

CHAPTER 8

Broken Promises

So do not fear, for I am with you; do not be dismayed, for I am your
God. I will strengthen you and help you; I will uphold you with my
righteous right hand.

—Isaiah 41:10 (NIV)

New Year's Evening

I T HAD BEEN a week and one day since Raymond's arrest. It
had been an unusually tranquil and untroubled time for the
Perez family, especially peaceful for Melissa. But that night would
prove that the rollercoaster ride Melissa thought was finally over
would resume again. It was almost ten o'clock that evening.
Melissa had done her best to stay off her feet, but with a one-
year-old baby, it proved challenging. Baby Sarah was then sound
asleep in her crib. Raymond was dressed in dark-gray slacks and
a baby-blue dress shirt. He spritzed some cologne on.

Melissa politely asked, "Where are you going?"

Raymond abruptly said, "Out. I'm going out," and he put his black leather jacket on.

Melissa, confused, asked, "Out where? Raymond, I'm especially not feeling good. And it's late. You never mentioned that you were going anywhere earlier."

"I don't have to tell you where I'm going or what I'm doing. What are you, my mother?" Raymond shouted.

"Oh wow. This is how you speak to me? You promised me last week after your arrest that you were a changed man and that it was a fresh start for us. You're not being a man of your word, Raymond," Melissa said.

She slowly sat up from the sofa and began walking into the kitchen. And suddenly, loud footsteps walked behind her. She looked back and *crack*. Melissa quickly fell hard to the ground backward.

"How many times do I have to tell you that I wear the pants in this marriage? You don't learn your lesson, do you?" Raymond shouted.

Melissa was laid out on the ground, crying with her hand over her mouth. Raymond had just punched her in the mouth. She wept and wept on.

"My tooth … it feels loose," Melissa cried out. "*Helllllp! Help!*"

Melissa burst out, calling for help, hoping that maybe one of the neighbors would hear her. She feared Raymond would really do it this time, that he would finally put an end to her life.

"Shut it!" Raymond then grabbed Melissa up from the floor and pressed his hand over her mouth. Melissa didn't stop; only now, her cries were muffled. Raymond tossed her onto the sofa. While standing over his weeping wife, he resumed holding his hand over her mouth.

"I told you to keep your mouth shut!" Raymond yelled. "Look

at me now. I got your mess all over me! You nag me to get a job; now I have one, and you're still nagging me."

Melissa just lay there crying.

"Look at you. You're fat. You're just a mess," Raymond said disrespectfully.

Melissa's eyes opened wide, and she began holding her belly. "Oh no! I think it's a contraction! No, no, no. I can't have the baby now!" Melissa cried loudly.

"Oh, calm down. There you go being dramatic again," Raymond said coldly. "I'm going out to make some money. Don't you dare question me again."

Raymond quickly changed his shirt, grabbed his jacket and keys, and then said, "If you call the police or you tell anyone about this, it's not gonna be good for you next time. Besides, you provoked me, like you always do," Raymond said sternly and then stormed out.

"Oh, Lord, please help me. Lord, guide me. Why have I put up with this? What is wrong with me? Please help me! Help me, Jesus!" Melissa continued to pray out loud while she cried.

The energy was evaporating from her body. Melissa very slowly reached for the telephone. She contemplated whether or not she should call someone. But there fear went again. It crept into her mind and heart like a thief. Fear quickly stole her peace of mind away—the peace of mind she had finally experienced this past week. Fear mocked her. It had a bad habit of taunting her. Melissa felt trapped in her own mind and spirit. Fear crushed her once again. She sat with the phone in her hand as the dial tone became a loud busy tone. Melissa's top lip was sorely cut open. She felt numb, completely frozen in her fear. Melissa once again gave in to it. She became a prisoner of fear. She kept hearing Raymond's voice in her head, "If you call the police or you tell

anyone about this, it's not going to be good for you next time."
She quickly put the telephone down.

Melissa went to go check on little Sarah, who surprisingly was still sound asleep. She was grateful for that. She walked out of the bedroom and into the bathroom. When she walked in, she saw her awful reflection in the mirror. She thought, *Who is that? Where is strong and confident Melissa?* What she was looking at was a fragile, broken woman with no self-esteem left. Her lip was surrounded by a bruise that looked purplish. She turned the cold water on and began gently splashing the water over her whole face. The light-pink water swirled in the sink and slowly went down into the drain as the cold water continued to run.

"Lord, thank You for this water. I know You are here with me," Melissa whispered under her breath so as not to wake up the baby.

After gently washing up, she looked up again at the mirror and still did not recognize herself. Disappointment was displayed on her face. Self-condemnation began settling in.

"This is completely my fault. I continue to stay here. I deserved this," Melissa said while looking up at the ceiling.

She started slowly walking into the kitchen to retrieve some ice for her lip. She put the ice in a freezer bag and applied it, but it burned. Melissa's belly was tightening up. It became painful for her. Maria was coming over the next morning to help Melissa at home.

"I can't let Mom see me like this. My mom will be so heartbroken." Melissa thought, *What possible excuse could I give her not to come over?* She didn't want to lie, but she also didn't want Maria knowing what had happened to her.

What if mom calls the police after seeing me this way? Melissa thought. So she picked up the phone and began dialing.

"Hello?" Maria answered.

"Ma … hi," Melissa said.

"What's the matter, honey? Is everything okay? It's almost eleven o'clock," Maria asked.

"Um, yeah, Ma ... Everything is fine." Melissa's voice trembled.

"Melissa, what's wrong?" Maria exclaimed.

"I'm fine," Melissa said.

"Where's Raymond?"

"Mom, don't worry. It totally slipped my mind that Raymond's mother said she was coming over tomorrow. Especially since, she hasn't seen Sarah in a couple of weeks. You've helped me so much already," Melissa said.

"No, sweetheart, it's fine. I can still come over for a bit."

"No!" Melissa interrupted. "I mean, no, Ma. I haven't spent any quality time with her and we actually need some catch-up time together alone. Do you know what I mean?" Melissa said.

"All right, love. But I'll come over the following day," Maria said.

"Aww, well, that's just it; she's actually coming over for a few days. Like I said, she also wants to have some bonding time with Sarah. I get to see you all of the time, especially since we live in the same neighborhood. It'll just be a few days," Melissa said.

"Okay, sweetheart, I'll call you in the morning. I'm happy you'll have help the next few days. If you need me, just call and I'll be right over. Get some rest," Maria said.

"Thanks, Ma. I love you."

"I love you too, mama," Maria said.

She hung up the phone.

"Lord, forgive me for being untruthful to my mother. I just can't let her see me this way. I don't want her to be heartbroken. I don't want her to be disappointed in me for being so weak. Please help me, God. I can't continue to live this way," Melissa prayed with tears dripping down her face. She was emotionally, spiritually, and physically worn out. She finally dozed off on the sofa.

CHAPTER 9

For the Love of Money

For the love of money is a root of all *kinds of* evil. Some people, eager for money, have wandered from the faith and pierced themselves with many griefs.

—1 Timothy 6:10 (NIV)

I T WAS 11:59 p.m. Two investigators pulled up in front of Mike's pharmacy. One of them had salt-and-pepper hair. He wore a black suit and had a hint of cigarette scent on him. The other was a little younger. He had dark-brown hair and was wearing a dark, navy-blue suit. He was about six-two. Inside of the pharmacy were Mike, Raymond, and a young woman. The young woman was blue-eyed and had bleached platinum-blond bob-styled hair. She was attractive and wearing a pink minidress and silver bling shoes.

One of the investigators said, "Good evening. How are you all doing tonight?"

Raymond nervously looked over at Mike.

Mike said, "Great. How can I help you?"

The investigator pulled a photo out of his inside jacket pocket. "Have you seen this girl?"

Mike became jittery. He seemed uncomfortable with the question.

"Ahh … no, actually, I've never seen her before," Mike answered.

The investigator turned the photo over to show Raymond and the young woman. Both shook their heads no.

Mike nervously asked, "Who is she? And what's the problem?"

"Well, this is a seventeen-year-old girl who has been missing for about a year. She lived in Long Island with her parents. We are private investigators that were hired by her family. The young lady's name is Emily. Her parents said she just didn't come home one day. There were a few people in this neighborhood who said they'd seen her in this area and in fact saw her in your pharmacy quite a bit," explained the investigator.

"Well, I've never seen her before," Mike quickly answered.

"I'm going to leave you my card. If you hear anything, please call me. But I'll be in touch again," the investigator said as they both exited the store.

Raymond quickly asked Mike, "What in the world was that all about?"

"Don't pay it any mind. Do you know how much that happens around here? I'm used to it already," Mike callously said.

The young woman who was with them suddenly said, "Mike, that was Sapphire, you know. Why did you—"

Mike quickly interrupted, "*Shut up!* You just shut your mouth! Don't you ever repeat that again!"

"Mike, you know her?" Raymond asked. "That girl was only seventeen years old."

"Ray, let's get one thing straight. I gave you a job, right?

Which also means I'm your boss! So you don't ask the questions. I do! Got it?" Mike shouted.

"Yeah, I got it," Raymond said.

For a quick moment, Raymond began thinking about little Sarah and how that missing girl could be his own daughter. Then a slight feeling of remorse began to settle in him when he thought how cruelly he'd also treated his wife. But he quickly snapped out of it when he thought about all of that money he was going to make. Those feelings of remorse quickly vanished away.

"Ray, you both stay here. I gotta go across the street for a sec. Lock the door behind me," Mike ordered.

"Okay," Raymond said.

Mike quickly walked out. The young woman sat down and sighed loudly.

"What's the matter?" Raymond asked her.

"I don't think I'm supposed to talk to you," the young woman said.

"Well, let me ask you this. How old are you anyway? Shouldn't you be home?" Raymond asked.

The young woman, with fear-filled eyes, appeared pensive for a few seconds. "Well, I just turned nineteen," she said.

"Nineteen?" Raymond exclaimed. "What are you doing in a place like this?"

"I work for Mike. I'm one of the girls that work for his dating service," the young woman replied.

"Do your parents know that you do this kind of work?" Raymond asked.

"I don't have parents. My dad left us when I was a baby, and my mom was a crack addict. I haven't seen my mom since I was fifteen. I've been on my own on these streets ever since. Mike was kind enough to take me in. If it weren't for him, I'd be dead or in jail."

"Oh wow!" Raymond said with a shocked look. "Aw, man, this is wrong on so many levels."

"Please don't tell Mike I told you any of this. I'm not supposed to talk to anyone," the young woman said.

"I won't. But tell me one more thing. I promise not to say anything."

"Okay," said the young woman.

"Sapphire, the girl who's missing, what happened to her?" Raymond asked.

The young woman clearly became uncomfortable. "Oh no, no, no. I'm not talking about that," she said.

"C'mon!" Raymond begged. "Just tell me; I won't say anything."

"Emily. Mike called her Sapphire. That was her alias working for the service."

"Okayyyy ... and?" Raymond asked.

"Well, she joined us last year. She ran away from home, said that her parents were too strict. Something about her story never made sense to me. But, anyway, Mike found her and also took her in. He fed her, gave her a warm place to stay, bought her a whole new wardrobe, and in return, she had to work for him, to pull her weight around here. He also got her cleaned up from the junk, you know. We do make good money."

"What? Aww, man. She's only seventeen though. So, if she's been missing for a year, that means she was only sixteen when she ran away from home," Raymond said.

"Well, Mike has a rule that we don't talk about our ages. As far as he's concerned, we are all supposed to say we are eighteen or older. I never knew Emily's real age. She never said, and I never asked. I did imagine she was young though. She had a baby face," the young woman said sadly.

"Well, do you girls just accompany men on dates, dinners, parties? I'm assuming it might involve more?" Raymond asked.

"Let's just say we do whatever makes our clients happy, no questions asked," the young woman said.

"Oh man," Raymond said as the color from his lips suddenly flushed out. "I thought he had grown women working for him ... not ..."

Suddenly, there was a hard knock at the door. Through the glass, Raymond could see that it was Mike. He opened the door.

"What are you talking about so much?" Mike yelled while looking at the young woman.

Raymond interrupted, "Nothing. We were just talking about how much money we're looking forward to making tonight. Are we ready?"

"Yeah, let's go make this bread," Mike replied. He rolled his eyes at both of them with suspicion.

CHAPTER 10

The Quiet before the Storm

Consider the blameless, observe the upright; a future awaits those
who seek peace.

—Psalm 37:37 (NIV)

THERE WAS A special place of peacefulness and beauty,
where a quiet calm rested deep within her soul. That was the
most alluring place for Melissa to reside in. It was a place that
she hadn't visited in a very long time. The name of that place was
serenity. Peace had been scarce in her family life with Raymond.
Two months had now come and gone since Raymond had laid a
finger on Melissa. Yesterday was Valentine's Day, and she spent
it alone with little Sarah. She had managed to pretty much stay
out of Raymond's way, and he hadn't been around much anyway
since starting his new job. Melissa had no real clue what kind of
work required him to be out all day and return sometimes a day
or two later with no explanation from him. But she didn't dare
question him out of fear she'd get knocked out again. It wasn't
worth it for her to take that chance.

The priorities of marriage and having a family had been placed on the back burner for him. Although it felt lonely going through her second pregnancy with no emotional support from Raymond, believe it or not, she was finally at peace. After all, Raymond was very unhappy about this second pregnancy. He had wanted Melissa to end the pregnancy when they first found out, but she refused to do that. Other than physical contact through abuse, which Melissa had endured in the recent past, Raymond would not touch her and never did in a loving or affectionate manner. He made it clear many times to her that it was necessary to withdraw from such affections to teach her a lesson for going through with the pregnancy. Melissa didn't miss having him around at all. She definitely didn't miss being put down and spoken to in a condescending manner. He was good at making her feel less than. And spending quality time with beautiful little Sarah was priceless. She also bonded with the baby that she had been carrying now for eight and a half months. Baby Diana was due March 1. There were only a couple more weeks to go. Melissa dreamed of looking into her baby's eyes to welcome her. She couldn't wait to meet her. She wondered and imagined what she would look like.

Melissa prayed, "Lord, thank You for sustaining me throughout these trying months. Thank You for this time of rest at home in order to have my baby when she is ready to come into this world. Thank You for protecting us. Amen."

Melissa was in constant contact via telephone with Mary, whom she had met at the hospital years before that awful night when she was beaten to a pulp. At that time, she was also newly married to Raymond and had received news that she was pregnant with little Sarah. Time did fly. Mary and Melissa had maintained a close friendship ever since then. Mary had become Melissa's confidante and voice of reason.

Mary planned on visiting her that day to catch up. It had been a few months since they'd seen each other. And it was the perfect time, since Raymond wasn't around.

The doorbell rang. Mary had finally arrived.

"Oh my goodness! Look at you!" Mary exclaimed. "You look so beautiful! Look at your beautiful belly!"

"It's so good to see you," Melissa said. "Come. Have a seat."

"So, how are you? How is the family?" Mary asked.

"Where do I begin? There's so much to catch up on. Everyone is okay. Thank God. Little Diana here ..." Melissa rubbed her belly. "She's very active. I'm guessing she can't wait to come out," she said and chuckled.

"Wow. I remember when you were pregnant with little Sarah. Your little family is growing," Mary said.

"Yes, it is," Melissa said with a pensive look. "Oh man, where are my manners? Would you like a cup of coffee? I just brewed a fresh pot," Melissa asked.

"Sure, I'd love a cup. Just black, no sugar, please."

"I also cooked tilapia sautéed in an onion marinade with asparagus and tomato and a side of angel-hair pasta," Melissa said.

"Yum! My favorite!" Mary exclaimed.

Little Sarah suddenly whizzed by, rattling her plush doll in her hand, happy as can be.

"Oh my goodness! Sarah is walking! Hi, sweetheart," Mary said to little Sarah.

"Yes, it's incredible. Once she discovered what she could do with those two little feet ... she's constantly on the go. It's hard to keep up with her at times," Melissa said and laughed. "I want the time to slow down. I remember when she first started to crawl."

"Melissa, you're so blessed. I'm at an age now that it's too late for me to bear children. I'm fine with it though. I have my beautiful niece and two nephews who are like my own. By the way, how's Raymond?"

"He's okay. I guess. He's hardly ever around these days," Melissa said.

"Oh? Why is that?" Mary asked.

"Well, he has a new job at some pharmaceutical company in the city," Melissa said.

"What does he do?" Mary asked.

"I honestly don't know, Mary," Melissa said with an embarrassed look.

"Melissa? What do you mean you don't know?" Mary asked. "Come on. Talk to me."

"Oh, Mary, it's complicated. I really don't know what he does. It makes me sick to my stomach because I'm afraid to ask him."

"Please tell me he doesn't get physical anymore with you," Mary said.

Melissa looked down in shame. She looked up at her and hesitated to respond.

"Melissa? No?" Mary asked with concern.

Melissa teared up, as her eyes welled up, she fought hard to hold the tears back; despite her efforts, they still came.

"Aw, honey," Mary said as she rose up from the sofa to hug Melissa.

Melissa cried in Mary's arms.

"I don't know what else to do, Mary. Just a couple months ago, the first night of this year, Raymond hit me. He punched me so hard that he busted my mouth open, and I panicked. What was I supposed to do? I'm pregnant and at high risk. I feel trapped. I'm scared, Mary. He's threatened if I try to leave him, that he'll kill me. He told me he's not living without Sarah."

"You can come stay with me. You don't have to live this way, Melissa," Mary said.

"I'm waiting to give birth. I've put everything on hold because I want to make sure the baby is fine. Believe it or not, the last two months haven't been so bad. Raymond rarely comes home. And the less time he spends here, the better it is for me and Sarah … and little Diana too," Melissa said.

"Yes, but at some point, you're going to have to find a resolution to this. Have you suggested marriage counseling?" Mary asked.

"Yes, I have. But he told me that he's not wasting his time or money on that," Melissa said, discouraged. "Honestly, Mary, I feel so bad saying this, but any love that I felt for him, I think is gone. He just beat it out of me. He makes me feel worthless."

"But you're not!" Mary exclaimed.

"I know, I know. It's just these circumstances, and not being able to do much physically has somewhat crippled me. Like I said, I'm waiting for little Diana to be born, and I will start making some moves," Melissa said. "I really can't continue on this way."

"I'm here for you, Melissa. You know that," Mary said.

"I know. Thank you, Mary. I appreciate it. I also feel bad for my parents. They have no idea what I've been going through."

"Why haven't you at least talked with your mom?" Mary asked.

"Oh no! It would break my mom's heart. And she tells my dad everything. I don't know how my dad would react. They're too old to have to deal with my problems," Melissa said.

"Melissa, you're potentially in danger and so are your babies," Mary said.

"Mary, you're the only one I've opened up to about what I've been going through. But I'm thinking of meeting with Pastor Delgado tomorrow morning," Melissa said.

"Oh?" Mary asked.

"Yes, I think I'm going to need to disclose some things. He's wonderful with prayer, and I can use a lot of it," Melissa said.

"Well, I think that's a great idea. It's okay to reach out for help, Melissa. So many people love you. I don't want anything to happen to you," Mary said and hugged Melissa.

CHAPTER 11

On Top of the World

Do not love the world or the things in the world. If anyone loves the world, the love of the Father is not in him. For everything in the world—the lust of the flesh, the lust of the eyes, and the pride of life—comes not from the father but from the world. The world and its desires pass away, but whoever does the will of God lives forever.

—1 John 2:15–17 (NIV)

THE SOUND OF the cash-counting machine was like music to Raymond's ears. They were rolling in lots of cash every week. After the first few weeks of working for Mike, Raymond realized that the pharmacy he began working for wasn't your typical pharmacy. He first saw a man who looked homeless walk in with a funny-looking prescription for oxycodone. Then another man walked in with a prescription for methadone. He started to notice a trend. Most, if not all of the customers did not appear to be working class or even just a parent coming in with a prescription for a child. It was a revolving door for the walking dead, who came in and out every day. It was the same familiar faces coming in for the same stuff. It soon struck Raymond that this wasn't your good ole neighborhood pharmacy; this was drug dealing in disguise. The pharmacy was just a front for Mike to conduct his business. Mike wasn't a pharmacist; he was a legally licensed drug dealer.

Raymond had a choice to do the right thing, but his love of the money he was making outweighed his need to do what was right. It didn't matter to him anymore. Mike's dating service was also fishy. Most of the girls who worked for him looked like they should be in high school, but Raymond figured the less he knew about the girls, the less he felt directly responsible. A lot of them had fake IDs and passports. Mike had an underground connection with someone who produced false documents. Raymond accidentally found out when he discovered and unlocked a drawer in Mike's back office with several girls' IDs.

Raymond convinced himself Mike was not hurting these girls. He'd taken them in and provided shelter and food for them. He justified it with a belief that there was nothing wrong with teenagers working—even though this wasn't a typical teenager's job. Besides, not all of the girls were teens anyway. And they all seemed happy and content. Raymond had now entered an entirely different world, and he had passed the point of no return. He knew too much, and by knowing all he did, he was also indirectly responsible, whether he believed that or not. But he didn't care. He became Mike's right-hand man. One of his jobs was to sell oxycodone and alprazolam pills at the club where the girls worked. He sold each pill of oxycodone for twenty-five dollars, and alprazolam, which on the street were known as Zannies or sticks, sold for ten to fifteen dollars a pill. Mike didn't allow the girls to use any drugs, except the Zannies. He wanted the girls to feel relaxed and carefree while working.

Diamond, the young, platinum blonde, walked in on Raymond counting the money.

"What are you doing back here?" Raymond asked loudly.

"Well, I'm the highest-paid girl here. I make a lot of money for you and Mike, don't I?" Diamond said.

"Hey, hey, hey, watch how you talk to me. You know that Mike has rules. No one back here while counting money. I'm responsible for it. So if any of it goes missing, it's my responsibility," Raymond said.

"I'm sorry, Ray. I just really need someone to talk to, and I'm reluctant to talk to Mike about it," Diamond said in a worried tone.

"All right, what is it? Make it quick," Raymond said.

"You know that I've been working for Mike for about three years, right?"

"Yeah, and?" Raymond said.

"Well, I've been saving up my money. I was thinking that maybe this isn't what I want to be doing for the next five years or even ever again. I've made enough money to put myself maybe through college."

"College?" Raymond laughed. "What are you gonna do for work while you go to school?"

"Well, I can get a normal job somewhere, maybe at a retail store or a supermarket. I need to start building a résumé for myself. I've always dreamed I'd be a teacher or maybe even some type of counselor," Diamond said excitedly.

"That sounds okay and all, but you're Mike's top girl. I'm not so sure he's gonna let you go that easy," Raymond said.

"Well, he always said that I can leave whenever I want to. And he doesn't know it, but I've been going to a really nice church," Diamond said.

"Church?" Raymond mockingly asked. "Are you serious?

God? Where was God when your father abandoned you? Or when your mom got hooked on crack cocaine and chose drugs over her own daughter? Think about it, if there was a God, you wouldn't be here right now, doing what you do," Raymond said sternly.

"Wow, okay. Ray, you just don't understand. When I go to this church, everyone is so nice and loving. I've learned so much about the unconditional love of God. No one ever took the time to teach me about the word of God. They talk with me, help me, love me, and there are no tricks up their sleeves. There's so much that I've learned," Diamond said.

"You sound crazy! You sound just like my wife. What is it with these religious fanatics that brainwash ya'll with such nonsense?" Raymond said.

"Ray, I'm not brainwashed. I'm saved. I gave my life to Jesus Christ. I feel an overwhelming sense of hope and peace—a hope that I never had before. I was always convinced that I wasn't good enough and didn't measure up. But my brothers and sisters at church have taught me that I am fearfully and wonderfully made. The problems that I've faced and the loss of my parents were traumatic, but I can use those experiences to help others. We live in the world which is filled with evil and traumas. Those things never come from God. I decided that I want to make a positive difference in this world. And Jesus has given me that hope," Diamond explained.

"What? Diamond, get outta here with that nonsense. You're on top of the world right now. You are the golden child of hustling. This is your forte. Why would you wanna give all of this up? Good luck with telling Mike that you're giving up making a few thousand dollars a week because you gave your life to Jesus. What a joke!" Raymond said and laughed.

"I'm confident that Mike will be okay with my decision. And as far as being on top of the world, before I was saved, I didn't feel like I was on top of the world. I felt burdened by it. I felt a sense of hopelessness and lived in constant fear every day. But no amount of money in this world can pay for what I know and feel now. I know that I will live in paradise for eternity with my father in heaven. I now live without shame and without condemnation because I know that I am forgiven. I received the gift of grace, which is offered to all of us. I live with the knowledge that God never stopped loving me, even after all of the mistakes I've made. I ran further away from Him because of the lies I chose to believe, but God ran after me. He found me, and He saved me. Ray, you should come one day with me to see what I mean," Diamond said.

"No, thanks, Diamond. You can keep your God to yourself. I'm good," Raymond said. "I don't go to church with my own family. Why would I go with you?"

"By the way, my name is not Diamond. My real name is Donna. You can call me Donna from now on."

"You'll always be Diamond to me," Raymond said and laughed.

"I can't wait to get out of this business. I don't want to wind up like Emily."

"What did you say?" Raymond asked, shocked.

"I meant that Emily was a lost soul. She had so much potential, and then she was nowhere to be found. It makes me sad because she was my friend."

"You talk too much! If Mike heard you mention Sapphire, he would have a fit. No more talk about her, okay?" Raymond said.

"Okay."

"So when are you gonna tell Mike about your new epiphany?" Raymond asked as he shook his head.

"I think maybe tonight. I can't do this type of work anymore," Diamond said.

"Well, like I said before, good luck with that," Raymond said.

CHAPTER 12

The Meeting

> But for those who are self-seeking and who reject the truth and follow evil, there will be wrath and anger. There will be trouble and distress for every human being who does evil: first for the Jew, then for the Gentile.
>
> —Romans 2:8–9 (NIV)

TIME CREPT ON the clock as Diamond waited for Mike to show up at the store. She was extremely anxious. She nervously nibbled on her thumbnail. Finally, she heard the sound of the door opening. It was Mike.

"Hey, what's up?" Mike asked. "What's so urgent? It's not like you to text me so much in one day, unless there's a problem. What is it that you want to talk with me about?"

"Well, can we go sit in your office?" Diamond asked.

"Yeah, but where's Ray?" Mike asked.

"He said he was picking up that money for you from the last job," Diamond explained. "He said he'll be right back."

"Ah, right. Okay. Make this quick. We have a lot of work to do tonight," Mike said.

"Well … uh, how can I put this?" Diamond asked nervously.

"C'mon, Diamond! What?" Mike said loudly.

"Okay. Um. Do you remember when you said to me that I could walk away from this anytime?" Diamond asked.

"Yeaaaah, why?" Mike asked sarcastically.

"Well, it's time that I leave the business, Mike. I want to thank you so much for everything you've done for me. I'm so grateful to you," Diamond said.

"What? Nah, nah, nah. You're not walking away that easily. What is it? Did someone else offer you something? Are you gonna work for Jamal over on the west side?" Mike asked.

"No, Mike. It's nothing like that. I'm out of this business for good. I'm going to college," Diamond said.

"Are you kidding me? College? You don't even have a high school diploma. And who's filling your head with bad ideas? You're gonna spend thousands of dollars on an unnecessary college education, then what? Work for an entry-level job, making an entry-level salary? Becoming a slave to corporate America, making chump change? You're not doing that!" Mike exclaimed.

"I took GED classes during the day and just received my diploma. Ray was right," Diamond said.

"What do you mean 'Ray was right'?" Mike asked. "Are you talking to Ray? Didn't I tell you, you talk to me *only*?"

"It's not Ray's fault. I approached him. He pretty much tried to convince me not to leave either. He said I have it good here with you," Diamond said.

"Well, Diamond, if it's money, you can get a bigger cut, okay? Enough with this nonsense! We gotta get to work," Mike said while he attempted to walk away.

"No, Mike. I'm serious." Diamond gently placed her hand on

his chest to grab his attention. "This isn't about the money. No one filled my head with anything. Mike … I gave my life to Jesus Christ," Diamond said.

Mike began hysterically laughing. He laughed so hard that tears built up and streamed down his face.

"Uhhhh, Diamond!" Mike continued to laugh obnoxiously. He tried to gather his composure. Diamond just looked at him in disbelief, stone-faced.

"Diamond, this is a good one. Sweetheart, this is by far the funniest thing I've heard. Jesus Christ? Now I know you've lost it," Mike said. "Stay off the Zannies for a few days. And remember, you are no church girl." He continued to laugh.

"Mike, I'm not joking. I'm not working tonight, and I'm not working for you anymore. I'm really out," Diamond said seriously.

"You forget that I know a lot of people. Stop this nonsense, Diamond. You're not going anywhere, understand me?" Mike said.

"Are you threatening me? Mike, you do know a lot of people. But you forget that I know a lot about you and what you do here. And I'm also the only one who knows what really happened to Sapphire," Diamond said.

Rage filled Mike's eyes. He rushed toward Diamond and tightly wrapped his hand around her neck.

"Now, you're threatening me! Don't you ever! Don't you dare, Diamond! No one knows who you are, and if you were gone, no one would even notice," Mike said as he released his hand from her neck.

Diamond began breathing hard. She said, "I'm not threatening you, Mike. I promise, you won't ever hear from me again. I will never tell. I just want to be set free. I just want to live a normal life," she pleaded.

"Okay, Diamond. This is what you really want? Then you

owe me one more job tonight. And you're free to go after that. No strings attached. Deal?" Mike said.

"Really?" Diamond asked with doubt.

"Yes, really," Mike said with silent rage in his eyes. "I gotta go meet with someone. I'll be back in about an hour. Tell Ray to call me as soon as he gets in."

"Okay, Mike," Diamond answered.

Minutes after Mike left, Raymond returned to the store. He saw Diamond sitting at the counter, crying.

"What happened?" Raymond asked.

"Ray, you were right. Mike was so upset. He said I'm not going anywhere," Diamond said.

"I told you," Raymond said. "What did he say?"

"It's too long to get into it. He said he'd let me go after one more job tonight. But I have to tell you something, Ray," Diamond said desperately.

"What is it?" Raymond asked.

"But first please promise me that you will not say a word?" she begged.

"Okay, I promise," Raymond said.

"No, really, Ray. You must *really* promise me. My life depends on it," Diamond said.

"Your life? Mike is a little nuts, but he would never harm any of you girls," Raymond said.

"Forget it, Ray!"

"Wait! Yes, I promise. I won't say anything. Just tell me," he said.

"Do you remember Sapphire? The girl who's missing?" she asked.

"Yeah?"

"Well, I wasn't completely honest when I said to you that I didn't know what happened to her," Diamond said.

"What are you saying? Get to it!" Raymond said.

"Sapphire got all cleaned up from the junk. When Mike found her, he helped her quit it altogether. She was doing great. But I guess after a while, working for this business was getting to her. No one knew, but she was secretly back on the stuff. Long story short, one night, Mike went in the back looking for Sapphire to take her out on a job and found her dead with a needle stuck in her arm. Mike panicked and rolled up her body. I don't know what he did with her body after that," Diamond said, trembling. She began to weep. She couldn't stop. "I knew. But Mike said if I ever tried calling the cops or told anyone, that I would never be found."

Raymond's face went pale. His lips had no color. "What?"

"Ray, I'm doing one more job for him tonight. If anything happens to me, please tell someone," Diamond said. "My friends at the church have somewhat adopted me as one of their own. They're my only family now. Here's the number to my church, just in case," Diamond said.

"I don't know what to say. You just threw me a lot of information here. Diamond, this is a huge allegation you're making," Raymond said.

"It's not an allegation! It's the truth! I begged him to call the police or an ambulance. I told him it wasn't his fault that she overdosed. But she was also missing, and he didn't want to get pinned with kidnapping. I mean, she did stay on her own willingly. I also didn't know Sapphire was underage when she came to us. But I should've known. I was only sixteen myself when I was found by Mike too. I only found out the night the two investigators came in and revealed her true age," she explained.

"I wish you didn't tell me this. What am I supposed to do with all of this?" Raymond asked.

"Ray, all I'm asking is if, God forbid, something happens to me, please do the right thing. Okay?"

They heard the sound of a car pulling up. Raymond looked out of the window.

"Shhh! Be quiet. He's back," Raymond said.

CHAPTER 13

The Counselor

For lack of guidance a nation falls, but victory is won through many advisers.

—Proverbs 11:14 (NIV)

EARLY MORNING LIGHT glistened through the white blinds. The clouds were gray and gloomy. The morning actually looked like late afternoon. There was a messy, unfolded blanket on the couch that hadn't been there when Melissa went to bed the night before. It looked like Raymond had maybe sneaked in during the wee hours of the night and slipped away before sunrise. Despite that fact, Melissa awoke refreshed and at peace. As long as she had no confrontations with him, she was out of the line of fire. She began feeling a little uneasy about the idea of meeting with Pastor Delgado. She was prepared to finally reveal the torment she had endured the last few years with him. Maybe Pastor could help save their marriage. Melissa prayed night after night for things to turn around for the better. She dreamed of bringing little Diana into the world to live in a home that was a sanctuary instead of a war zone.

A couple of hours passed. Melissa arrived with baby Sarah in her stroller. Even though their church was only about five minutes away, she took a cab there just in case. Pastor Delgado was aware of Melissa being on bed rest, so when she arrived, he was in front of the church waiting.

"Hello, dear. How are you?" Pastor Delgado asked as he helped Melissa with little Sarah into the church.

"Hi, Pastor Delgado. It's so good to see you. Thank you so much for meeting with me today," Melissa said with gratitude.

"Hello, Sarah. And look at you, almost in the home stretch, huh?"

"Yes," Melissa said with one hand supporting her lower back. "Baby Diana can't wait to be home. She's kicking away in here. I can't wait either," she said with a smile.

Melissa continued to follow Pastor to his office. His office was absolutely stunning. It had a Greek pillar-like trim around the doors. The crown molding on the ceiling was a beautiful glistening gold color, and the walls were bright white. The furniture was made of beautiful dark mahogany wood. Over to the right of his desk on the wall was an exquisite gold cross. To the left was a shelf with an array of books. On Pastor's desk were his Bible, a few stacks of documents and sermons neatly placed in the corner, and brass and gold pen holders.

"Have a seat, Melissa," Pastor Delgado said. "So, how are you, dear? And Raymond? I have not seen him in a very long time."

"Uhh. There's so much to say. Where do I start?" Melissa said.

"Well, I have the whole morning, dear. There is no rush," Pastor Delgado said.

"Okay, well, little Sarah has been just great. She's doing so much now. She's walking and even saying a couple of words. It's pretty amazing to see her reach these milestones. As for Raymond, well, actually, that's why I'm here today, Pastor. Raymond and I have not been good at all," Melissa said.

"I'm sorry to hear that. No wonder I haven't seen him attend worship with you and Sarah on Sundays. Tell me what's going on. I'd like to help."

"Well ..." Melissa looked down at her fidgety hands. "I honestly don't know where to begin. I also feel guilty talking with you about it. I am quite embarrassed," Melissa said as she began to bite her nails.

"You don't have to be embarrassed, Melissa. This is part of my job. I counsel married couples all of the time. Also, please know that whatever is spoken about here is completely confidential," Pastor Delgado assured her.

"Pastor ... Raymond beats me. He's been hitting me for years," Melissa said.

"Melissa, I'm so sorry!" Pastor Delgado said with a shocked look on his face. "Have you reached out for help? What about your parents? I think it's best you stay with them until Raymond gets help."

"No, I haven't. It's complicated, Pastor. I don't want to burden or worry my parents. And the first time he hit me was three months into our marriage. That time is also when I found out that I was pregnant with baby Sarah. Pastor, he promised that it would be the last time he'd hit me. I forgave him. And love covers all shame, right?"

"Wow. You've been carrying around this burden for quite some time. God doesn't want you to be burdened. He doesn't want you to suffer. It also sounds like Raymond may need professional help. But I can also arrange for counseling for you both here at the church," Pastor Delgado said. "How often is the abuse?"

"The signs were there when we were first dating. He was a bit controlling at first. I thought it was just him being overprotective of me. I thought it was endearing at first. But then, he would tell me things like I was gaining weight or he didn't like what I was wearing and so on. After we got married, he first got physical by grabbing me. But it wasn't until three months after, he just lost it on me. I honestly thought I was going to die that night. When I was pregnant with Sarah, he would pinch me and slap me. And as far as counseling, I can't do that, Pastor. Raymond would kill me if he knew I was even talking with you about this," Melissa said desperately.

"Oh my word, I'm so sorry, dear. How is he with little Sarah?" Pastor Delgado asked.

"Ironically, he's good to her. He is affectionate with her at times and also protective of her, but he also doesn't hesitate to hit me or yell at me right in front of her either. She's frightened when he does that. I don't want my babies watching this. I don't want my girls growing up thinking that it's okay for a man to be abusive with his wife. My heart is so broken," Melissa said with tears welling.

"Okay. I won't tell him that we spoke about this. But I strongly suggest you stay with your parents for now. And how about, once you have the baby, I want you to start coming Wednesday nights to our women's support group. It is confidential, and you can bring the babies with you. I have one of the girls from our youth group here that does babysitting," Pastor said.

"Thank you. I think I'd like that," Melissa said.

Then there was a knock on the door.

"Come in," Pastor Delgado said.

The door slowly opened, and a man peeked in.

"Ahh, John, come in," Pastor Delgado said as he motioned with his hand, welcoming him.

The handsome gentleman walked in. He had short, dark hair, buzzed on the sides with a little more hair on the top of his head. He was about six feet one inch and had light-brown eyes and a tan complexion. He was obviously physically fit with a strong build. He wore blue jeans with a black crew-neck shirt.

"Hey, Melissa, this is one of our volunteers here. He works part-time for our youth ministry for men. This is John Parris." Pastor Delgado then looked over at John. "John, this is Melissa Perez."

"Nice to meet you, Melissa," John said politely as he shook Melissa's hand. "You look familiar."

Melissa shyly smiled. "Nice to meet you too. Yes, I think I've seen you around here at the church too," Melissa said.

"Pastor, so sorry to have interrupted your meeting. But we need your opinion quickly. It's regarding the upcoming retreat for the men's group. It will only take a couple of minutes. I'm so sorry, Melissa," John said as he made eye contact with Melissa.

"No worries. You go on ahead. I have all day," she said.

"Hey, would you like to join us? I can show you some artwork that a couple of the guys did here. We're donating all of the artwork to a few local hospitals," John said.

"I'd love to, John. Only thing is I'm supposed to be on bed rest and not really supposed to be out and about," Melissa said.

"How many months are you?" John asked.

"Actually almost nine. I'm due in another couple weeks," Melissa said.

"Well, congratulations. Hey, why don't I bring a couple of the art pieces here? You just relax. Stay seated. I'd actually like some feedback. Do you mind?" he asked. "Is it okay with you, Pastor?"

"Of course it's fine. Melissa is actually some kind of designer in the city. She'd be perfect to ask for feedback," Pastor Delgado said.

"Sure," Melissa said with a bright smile. Her smile had been buried for years. It then painted a glimmer of hope at that very moment.

"Okay, I'll be right back," John said as he began to walk out with Pastor Delgado.

"Thank you, dear. We won't be long," Pastor Delgado chimed in.

CHAPTER 14

The Devil's Trap

Let no one deceive you with empty words, for because of such things God's wrath comes on those who are disobedient. Therefore do not be partners with them.

—Ephesians 5:6–7 (NIV)

BACK AT THE pharmacy, Mike and Raymond were preparing for the long day ahead of them. Mike's cell phone rang.

"Hello … Yeah, what's up, bro? … What? … So are you bringing me the shirts or the brown shoes?" The person continued to converse with Mike. "Wait. What? … I thought it wasn't happening until the following week? … Okay … okay. I'll make it happen … Give me twenty minutes. I'll ring you back," Mike said in a hurry.

"What's up, bro? Everything okay?" Raymond asked.

"Nah, man. Everything is not okay," Mike said.

"What's up?" Raymond asked.

"What's up is that I got two bricks of heroin coming in. It wasn't supposed to come in for another couple of weeks. And my mill isn't gonna be ready at my usual spot until then. I need a place to cut the stuff up and have it ready in a week," Mike said.

"Hey, I got an idea!" Raymond exclaimed.

"What?" Mike asked, annoyed.

"You know things between me and Melissa have been messed up. She can't stand the sight of me, bro. I've been wanting to fix up our apartment for a while, but with work and all, I just don't have the time," Raymond said.

"Yeah, what does that have to do with this right now?" Mike shouted.

"Well, what I'm saying is you can use my apartment for the weekend to cut up the stuff," Raymond suggested.

"Yeah, how do you suppose we can pull that off when your wife and kid live there?" Mike said.

"Well, that's just it; I'll tell her that I'm gonna renovate our apartment for her, finally sand the floors like she wanted, fix up the baby's room. And I can probably really convince her by telling her that I'll build her a closet just for her shoes. *But* obviously with her being pregnant and my baby daughter, they would have to stay with her parents for the weekend," Raymond explained.

"Bro! That's a great idea! You think she'll go for it?" Mike asked.

"Listen, if I let you use my apartment, all I ask is that you get your guys to really do the stuff for me. The closet should be easy and sanding the floors too. It will only take about two days for the renovations. What do you think? Deal?" Raymond said.

"You got a deal! But we need like five days, three days to cut the stuff up and two days to do your renovations. Your apartment isn't that big, is it?" Mike asked.

"Nah, it isn't. It's a three-bedroom apartment. But I only need the baby's room fixed up. The closet is gonna be in our bedroom. I think we can pull it off," he said.

"Hey, Ray, thanks for looking out. You gotta get your family out by tomorrow though. This gotta get done right away. And listen, I got a deal in return for you," Mike said.

"Anything for you, bro," Raymond said.

"Since I'm gonna have my guys build a nice walk-in shoe closet for your lady, I'm actually short one spot for the stash. I was thinking maybe I can have the guys build a secret trap within the new shoe closet as a stash spot," he said.

Raymond's face suddenly got really serious. "What? Are you serious? A trap? What if she notices?" he asked nervously.

"Nah, she won't. I've been doing this for a long time, Ray. Don't you trust me? I'm no idiot. The trap will big enough to stash the cash and some of the stuff. Once it's built, you'll see what I mean. Now … the deal is, if you let me use your place as one of my stash spots, I'll give you a bigger cut on all the jobs—3 percent more. So? Yes or no?" Mike asked.

"You got a deal. I trust you," Raymond said.

Two Hours Later

Raymond inserted the key in the top lock. Click. He put the key in the bottom lock and opened the apartment door. "Melissa! Melissa?" Raymond yelled out.

Raymond looked around, but no one was home.

"Where are they?" he thought out loud.

Raymond pulled his cell phone out. He began dialing to call Melissa's phone. There was a sudden clicking noise. It was the door.

"Raymond," Melissa said, startled. "What are you doing here?"

"What am I doing here?" Raymond laughed sarcastically. "I live here, remember?"

"No, I meant since you've been working so much, I guess I wasn't expecting to even see you at all today," Melissa said.

"And where were you? Aren't you supposed to be on bed rest?" Raymond asked.

"Well, I needed to stop at the church quickly. I just had to drop something off," Melissa said.

Raymond almost forgot why he was there in the first place. He had to get himself in her good graces. So his tone immediately changed.

"Awww, that's so nice, baby. Listen. I wanted to talk with you," Raymond said.

"Oh?" She looked nervous.

"Yeah. Listen, I've been terrible to you. I know I haven't been around much. Just trying to be the provider like you wanted, right? Well, first I want to say I'm sorry."

Melissa looked at him in disbelief as he continued, "I want to make it up to you and little Sarah. You know how you've been asking for the floors to be sanded?"

"Yes?" Melissa asked reluctantly.

"Well, I hired a team of guys to come here tomorrow. I'm gonna have them build you a walk-in shoe closet and also fix up the baby's room. What do you think?" Raymond asked.

"Well, um … Wow, this is all so sudden." Melissa became suspicious. "Why now? After all of this time?"

Raymond's blood began to boil. But he forcibly kept his composure. He remembered that this had to be done sooner than later.

"Like I said, baby, I want to make it up to you. You're gonna love it when it's done. There are gonna be a bunch of guys working here. There will be debris and dust all over. I can't have you and Sarah stay here. You're gonna have to stay with your parents until at least Monday or even Tuesday," Raymond explained.

"Raymond, I appreciate so much that you want to do this for us. I'm happy, but you picked such a challenging time to do this. I'm on bed rest," Melissa said.

"Yeah, baby, but I don't know when I'll have the opportunity or money to do this later on. Now is the perfect time. Besides, your folks have that extra bedroom. It's comfortable enough. And you'll have your mom there to help you," Raymond said.

"Yeah, I guess you're right. All right, let me call them. Thank you for doing this, Ray," Melissa said as she remembered how Pastor Delgado had told her that morning he'd be praying for them. Melissa hoped that this was a sign of an answered prayer.

While Melissa was about to call her mom, Raymond stepped out in the hallway.

He began dialing Mike's number.

"Yeah, Mike. We're in! I'll have her outta here by like ten tomorrow morning. Tell your guys to get here by noon. We should be good to go. I'm outta here in about an hour. See you soon." He hung up.

Raymond then walked back into the apartment.

"So? Did you call?"

"Yes, they said it was fine. I'm very surprised. You caught me off guard with all of this," Melissa said.

"It will be worth it. Trust me. The guys will be here around eleven tomorrow, so we'll leave before then. I'll drop you and Sarah off. I gotta run. I'll be back later. Gotta job to do," he said hurriedly.

"Wait. I just got home. Sarah and I haven't seen you," Melissa said.

"Sorry, I gotta go. I'll call you later," he said coldly.

Melissa's intuition kicked in. Something didn't feel right, but she had to hang on to hope that maybe this was a slight turn for the better.

CHAPTER 15

Enemy in My Own Home

A man's enemies will be the members of his own household.
—Matthew 10:36 (NIV)

THE FOLLOWING MORNING was setup day at Raymond's apartment. With Melissa and baby Sarah out of their way, they were able to set up shop. A crew of a few guys carried in four long tables, big black garbage bags, and another bag with all the materials they needed to get the job done. Mike had a work crew of about ten guys come in. Their jobs were going to be cutting up the drugs and then packaging and stamping them. Every person had to remove his clothing and wear scrub-like gear. They were also ordered to put all devices, including cell phones, in a bag.

"Let's go! Let's go! Let's go! Every minute counts here! You all know no one leaves here for three days. No phone calls, no nothing. Raymond will be going out to bring food for ya'll. If anybody got a problem with that, say it now," Mike shouted as the crew of guys all looked at each other and remained silent.

"All right, now that we got the rules outta the way, we're gonna use the rear bedroom. The windows gotta be all covered and taped up. Use the black bags for that. Ray, go have them bring three tables to the back with all the stuff, the blenders, lamps, and weight scales. Then bring one table to the kitchen. That's where we're gonna do all the stamping," Mike ordered.

"Mikey, where am I setting up the police scanner?" Raymond asked.

"Set it up in the living room, so we can all hear it. And last but not least, don't forget to reinforce the front door. Okay, let's get to it," Mike said.

"Mike, how many lookouts do you want?" Raymond asked.

"Okay, I'm gonna need four of you as lookouts. Ray will wait in here with the others while I go out to bring the stuff in. When all of it is inside, I'll assign who's doing the cutting, who's packaging, and who's stamping. I want the stuff stamped, 'Godzilla,'" Mike said.

"Okay, let's go!" Raymond said.

After a long five days away from home, Melissa anxiously waited for Raymond to pick her and baby Sarah up. She couldn't wait to see their newly renovated apartment. The truth was Raymond really hadn't done much around their home, so this was especially out of character for him. Yet, she still remained grateful.

"Mom … Dad, thank you so much for letting us stay with you guys. You've been so good to us," Melissa said.

"Of course, sweetheart. We missed having you around here. You've been cooped up in that apartment for a while. I guess it all worked out," David said.

"I wonder what's taking Raymond so long? He said he'd be here by now," Melissa said.

"Do you want me to take you home?" David asked.

"No, Dad, you've done so much already. He should be here soon," Melissa said.

Back at Their Apartment

"C'mon! Let's wrap this up!" Raymond shouted at the guys cleaning up after adding the closet in his bedroom.

The floors had been sanded the day before. The baby's room was freshly painted in a pale-pink color, white crown molding was added, and a pretty light-gray rug had also been installed. The tables that were used for cutting up the drugs and packaging still needed to be taken out of the apartment. Mike hired a cleanup crew to speed things up.

"Guys, let's go! Let's go! We got somewhere to be!" Mike continued to shout at them.

"So, didn't I tell you that you wouldn't be able to detect the secret trap?" Mike asked.

"Yeah, you were right. It's incredible. No one would ever find it. It's well-built," Raymond agreed.

Mike then entered the closet to show Raymond how the trap worked. Inside of the closet was a stair-like construction. He reached for two small knobs at the very bottom part of the steps. He turned one knob to the left, turned the other knob to the right, and then flipped a small light switch. Suddenly, a slight humming, mechanical sound occurred and simultaneously caused the top step to rise. It was the trap door that had just opened. Raymond noticed a medium-sized storage crawl space inside. He observed bags of rice and coffee at the very bottom.

"Mike, why are there bags of rice and coffee inside the trap?" Raymond asked, confused.

"Ray, you're a new jack for real." Mike laughed as he continued to explain, "The bags of coffee are to disguise the odd smell that heroin has, and the bags of rice are to absorb the humidity."

"Ahhh, got it," Raymond said.

"Okay, so we're gonna leave half of the stuff that we prepped this week in the trap. Bring it with you Thursday night, cool?" Mike said.

"Got it. I gotta go get Melissa. Can you lock up when you all leave? I'll be back with her in about twenty minutes. You think you'll be outta here by then?" Raymond asked.

"Yeah, man, we'll be out in about ten minutes. But, hey, do you think your lady will like what we did here?" Mike asked.

"She better like it, or she's gonna get slapped upside her head." Raymond laughed.

Mike began to laugh too.

"Well, I'll catch you later," Mike said.

"Later," Raymond said.

Thirty Minutes Later

Raymond gave Melissa the honor of opening the door. At first sight of the apartment, she noticed how beautiful the hardwood floors looked. They were a glistening caramel color. They looked brand new.

"Oh my goodness! The floors are amazing!" Melissa gasped. "Raymond, they did a wonderful job!" she said as she approached to hug him.

Raymond took notice but quickly began walking toward the bedrooms, totally avoiding her hug.

"Come! Wait until you see the baby's room," he said.

Melissa gasped again and gave him a wide smile. "Wow! The room looks like something out of a magazine! Raymond!" Melissa exclaimed.

"Didn't I tell you?" Raymond said. "And last, but not least ..."

As Melissa walked into their bedroom, on the right side of it, where there used to be a wall, were two oriental-style sliding doors to a new walk-in closet. Inside of the closet were built-in lighting, new shelves, and three rows of boxed steps for her shoes.

"I don't know what to say. You did a fantastic job! Thank you so much!" Melissa said.

"Don't say I don't do anything for you. I better not get any slack from you when I can't come home sometimes," Raymond said in an arrogant voice.

"Raymond!" Melissa said with confusion on her face.

"Raymond what? Don't start!" Raymond shouted.

"Really? So that was what this was all about? A nice gesture to keep me quiet?" Melissa asked.

"Melissa, you need to stop. Your mouth is gonna get you in trouble. Do not provoke me!" Raymond shouted again.

With a look of dismay, once again, Melissa slowly walked away from Raymond.

"Are you walking away from me? How many times have I told you that you don't walk away from me?" Raymond yelled with rage.

"Excuse me, Raymond. I just need to use the bathroom. Is that okay with you?" Melissa asked softly.

"Go ahead. I gotta go anyway," Raymond said as he muttered more words of anger under his breath.

A door then slammed. Melissa sat on her bed and began crying.

"I knew it. I knew this was too good to be true," Melissa cried out loud. "He's never going to change."

Melissa began to pray.

Any hope that Melissa had for Raymond changing was completely gone for good. Baby Sarah was sound asleep in her crib. Melissa lay on her bed sobbing. Here she went again. After two months, with no real contact with her husband, and after their first real encounter after so much time, he was still the same old Raymond as before. Melissa had an uncanny ability to imagine wonderful events and plans for her future. She lay there and could think of nothing good except her children.

"Lord, please help me. Give me guidance. I know You're with me, but You are silent. I feel lost and confused. Lord, I pray that baby Diana is born healthy. I pray that You give me the courage to do what's right. Because at this moment, I just don't know what I'm gonna do."

CHAPTER 16

Missing

Enemies disguise themselves with their lips, but in their hearts they harbor deceit.

—Proverbs 26:24 (NIV)

AT THE PHARMACY, it was just another day of business as usual. Raymond had been lining everything up for Mike. One tiny notion kept him distracted. He puzzled over where Diamond had been. Raymond kept calling her on the cell phone, but the calls continued to go straight to her voice mail. It seemed that her phone might have been shut off. And this time, an automated message pronounced that her voice-mail box was full. He hadn't heard from her in almost a week, which was unusual. They had been in contact almost every day, since day one. The last conversation he had had with her was when she asked for Raymond's advice on how to approach Mike. Raymond remembered that she had given him the telephone number to her friends at the church. Deep down inside, something gnawed at him. In his mind, he battled over whether he should call the number or not. He considered that maybe Diamond had merely taken off because she couldn't face Mike with her truth. There was only one way to find out. The phone continued to ring.

Precisely as Raymond was ready to hang up, a warm, comforting female voice answered, "Hello?"

"Ah, yeah, hi. I'm looking for Dia ... Donna," Raymond said, correcting himself.

"May I ask who's speaking?" the woman asked as her tone changed from warm to suspicious.

"I'm a friend of hers. I haven't seen or spoken with her in about a week. She gave me this number in case I needed to reach her," Raymond said.

"And what is your name, sir?" the woman asked.

"My name is Ray," he answered.

"Ahhh, yes. I know who you are. Donna has told me about you. Well, I'm glad that you called. We are all concerned about her. She's been coming here for almost a year, and she's never missed a service on Sunday. She's also in our youth ministry group and already missed two meetings," the woman said.

"Umm, oh wow. Okay. And what's your name, ma'am?" Raymond asked.

"My name is Micaela. If we don't hear from her soon, we are going to call the police. I understand that you're one of the gentlemen she worked for. I'm also aware that she was leaving that job," she said.

"Okay, Micaela. Let me see if I can locate her. I'm sure she's fine. Can I call you later?" Raymond asked.

"Yes, sir. Please do. We are all very worried. Donna has never been late or missed any meetings. And she always calls. If I don't hear back from you later on today, I'm going to file a missing persons report," she said fervently.

"Okay," Raymond said and quickly hung up.

Raymond turned around and was startled to see Mike standing at the door.

"Who were you talking to?" Mike asked angrily. "I've been calling you all morning."

"How long were you standing there?" Raymond asked.

"I asked you first. Who were you talking to?" Mike asked loudly this time.

"It was Diamond's friend from the church. She was asking if I'd seen her," Raymond responded.

"Diamond's friend from the church? How did she get your number?" Mike asked.

"I don't know. She must've given them my number," Raymond lied.

"So what do you have to do with Diamond? It's nobody's business where she is. She's a big girl and can take care of herself," Mike shouted.

"I mean, c'mon, Mike. She just disappeared. It's not like her not to be around or at least call. Mike, what happened the last time you guys spoke?" Raymond asked.

"Excuse me? Are you serious with that question? I'll tell you what happened the last time we spoke: *none of your business!* That's what! Diamond is not your business. She's mine. You work for me!" Mike shouted again.

"Listen, I do whatever you want me to do. And I'm grateful to you for work. Just want to know that she's good. She said she was doing one last job for you, and that was the last I heard from her," Raymond said.

"I'm gonna tell you one more time. Diamond is none of your concern. I don't know where she is! She quit. Who knows? Maybe she moved out of state. She's not my concern anymore. Now let's talk about the plan for tonight," Mike said.

Raymond didn't believe a word he said. He was a good liar

himself, and it takes one to know one. But there was nothing he could do right then. Raymond thought he could go look for her tomorrow. Suddenly, Raymond's phone began to ring. It was Melissa.

He answered, "What? What is it?"

"Ray, why does your friend Mike have a key to our apartment?" Melissa asked. "He scared me! How dare you give strangers keys to our home?"

"Wait a minute. Hold up! What? How did you meet Mike? What are you talking about?" Raymond said. "Mike was there?"

"Yes! Your friend opened the door to our apartment with Sarah and me here. I nearly called the police!" Melissa exclaimed.

"I'll take care of it. Going home soon," Raymond abruptly said.

"But, Raymond …" Melissa said.

But Raymond hung up on her.

"Mike! Mike!" Raymond hollered while he looked around for him.

He looked through the front glass door and saw him. He opened the door quickly.

"Mike!" he called out again.

Mike walked toward Raymond, who was standing in the doorway. The pharmacy was closed that day, so it was just the two of them inside.

"What happened?" Mike asked.

"Bro, how dare you go to my apartment with my family there! My apartment is off limits! And how did you get a key to my place?" Raymond said.

"First of all, tone it down! You and I had a deal! Your place is officially one of my stash spots now. So that means that if I need to go there to pick up or drop off, then that's what I'll do," Mike said. "And as for having the keys, I made a copy of your keys the day you left me with the crew to lock up. I assumed you knew that I needed the keys."

"Hold up! Hold up! Hold up! My place is a stash spot, but I never agreed for you to have a key to my apartment and especially for you to pop up whenever you want with my kid and wife there! Are you outta your mind? My wife is due any day now; she's on bed rest. And my baby daughter is there too!" Raymond said with outrage.

"Funny, 'cause you didn't have a problem having me build a trap in your wife's new closet that I had built for her. And I didn't see you complaining about all the cash you've been making. I kept calling you and got no answer, so I went over there looking for you," Mike explained.

"Well, this is gonna be a big problem for me. I need the keys back. I thought it was my job to pick up or drop off whatever needed to be stored at my place. I need those keys back," Raymond said harshly.

"I'm sorry, Ray. You can't get them back. When you agreed to work for me, I told you it's my rules. If you have a problem with that, then you can leave and be outta work again. Let's see how you gonna take care of your family now. Get this straight, Ray. You ain't nobody without me," Mike said maliciously.

Raymond's face reddened. His eyes filled with wrath, and his hands trembled, not out of fear, but out of fury.

"I gotta go get your stuff. I'll be back," Raymond said.

"Well, come right back. Remember, you gotta drop the girls off at their job. And then you're dropping my truck off at the garage uptown. I got someone that's gonna be waiting for you there at ten. You don't touch anything in the truck. You just drop it off, and they're gonna give you another car to take back with you. Call me on your way back," Mike said.

Raymond didn't respond or give him eye contact. He bolted

out of there. While driving on the FDR Highway back home, Raymond was driving about ninety miles per hour. He swerved in and out of traffic like a race-car driver. Drivers honked their horns, wondering who this crazy person driving on the road was. Raymond was swearing and cursing the whole way home.

CHAPTER 17

Worst Fear Comes to Light

What I have feared has come upon me; what I dreaded has happened to me.

—Job 3:25 (NIV)

AFTER HER ENCOUNTER with Mike that morning, Melissa was still pretty shaken up. She had even considered calling a locksmith to change the locks. It was then almost seven o'clock in the evening. She heard the rustling of keys outside of the door. It was Raymond. He walked in and slammed his keys on the table.

"Tell me what happened when Mike came into the apartment!" Raymond shouted.

"He just opened the door, like he lived here. He looked surprised to see me and asked where you were. Ray, why does this man have keys to our home?" Melissa asked, troubled.

"Listen! It's nothing! I lent him the keys, and I had to give him something. It's a misunderstanding, okay? Now tell me, did he go into any of the rooms or anywhere in the apartment?" Raymond asked with anger in his eyes.

With a puzzled look, Melissa said, "No, he didn't. Why would he go into any of the rooms? I wouldn't allow that. Ray, I'm concerned. We have a one-year-old baby, and baby Diana will be here any day now. I don't feel safe in my own home anymore," she said.

"What are you saying? I told you that you're not going anywhere! Understand me?" Raymond hollered.

"Am I wrong here? I can't live under these circumstances anymore. You're never around. Honestly, even though it's been peaceful around here, after this morning, that peace is completely gone. You put your family in harm's way, Raymond," Melissa said courageously.

"What did you just say?" Raymond asked with a blank stare.

"Ray, I don't know what you do. Your friend or boss, or whoever he was, gave me a bad feeling. I think I'm gonna talk with Mom and Dad. I'm gonna ask if Sarah and I can stay with them for a little while," Melissa explained.

"Oh no, you're not! You ain't going anywhere!" Raymond shouted as he charged at her.

"Raymond!" Melissa shrieked.

Raymond grabbed her by the throat, and she gagged. Melissa's face quickly reddened with tears flowing from her eyes. He charged at her with his hand still on her. Sarah began to cry. Raymond let go of Melissa, picked Sarah up, and brought her to her room. When Raymond returned to the living room, he glimpsed Melissa with the phone in her hand. As she began dialing, he dashed toward her, yanked the phone, and saw two numbers, "9" and "1," on the digital screen.

"Were you calling the police?" Raymond asked with rage.

With pure terror in Melissa's eyes, Raymond punched her in the center of her face. Melissa forcefully fell hard backward. She could barely get two words out from the shock of the blow.

She put her hand over her nose. She continued to feel his pressure against her body. As she lay on the ground sideways, Raymond just stood on and over her as he continued shouting, "I told you, keep your mouth shut!" Raymond had lost all control. "You were gonna call nine-one-one on me? Huh? While I'm out there making a living to support you? You're a mess!" Raymond shouted.

Melissa blubbered and whimpered. She tried calling out for help but gagged and suddenly coughed hard.

"The baaaby!" Melissa could barely say the words in a hoarse whisper.

"You were calling the police!" Raymond continued to yell. As he bent down, he gave her two last punches. Melissa lay there. Her face was obviously injured. Baby Sarah's cries were raw and intense.

She continued to cry out, "Mama! Mama!"

Sarah stood up in her playpen, crying out for Melissa.

Raymond looked at Melissa on the floor. "What have I done?" he said loudly as if he had snapped out of some kind of blind rage. Raymond went mad. He whispered, "I gotta get outta here. I wasn't here. My wife's been attacked." He was already concocting an alibi as if this were a random act of violence.

He took a chair from the dining room and smashed it. He quickly went into their bedroom and emptied out the drugs from the secret trap closet, but he left the money. He then locked it up and bolted out of the apartment.

Moments later, the neighbor went knocking on the door. She could hear the baby crying. She continued to knock.

"Raymond? Melissa? Anyone home?" The neighbor knocked a few more times. After no answer and listening to baby Sarah's cries, the neighbor called 911 from her cell phone.

The dispatcher answered, "Nine-one-one, what is your emergency?"

The neighbor, breathing heavily, said, "My neighbor, Melissa, I think she's in trouble!"

"Okay, what's going on? Where is your friend now?"

"Well, I heard loud noises, I heard her screaming, and now I only hear the baby crying. Melissa's not answering the door! Please hurry!"

"Okay, ma'am, I need for you to calm down. Where are you now?"

"I'm on Lauren's Place, Fifty-Five Lauren's Place in the Bronx, Apartment 2F. Please hurry! Something is wrong!" she yelped.

"Do you know if anyone else is in the apartment with them?" the dispatcher asked.

"No, I don't know! But Melissa is nine months pregnant! Please send someone! Hurry!"

"Did you just say she's pregnant?"

"Yes! She's pregnant!"

"Okay, ma'am, the police are on their way. Please stay calm. How old is her baby?"

"The baby is one year old, and she's still crying. She sounds scared. Oh no! Please hurry!" The neighbor's voice trembled.

"Ma'am, the police should be there very soon. Stay on the line with me."

"Oh please, God, let them be okay. Please hurry! The baby is crying. Where are they? What's taking them so long?"

"Please remain calm. They should be there any minute now."

"Thank God! They're here!"

"Are the police there, ma'am?"

"Yes, they're here." She hung up the phone.

Bam! Bam! Bam! Bam! The police banged on the door. "Hello! Is anyone home? Police! Open up!"

Sarah bellowed.

"No one's answering. I've been here the whole time knocking. My friend is nine months pregnant. She would never leave her baby alone," the neighbor said.

"Police! Open up!"

The police officer radioed in. "Central, this is sector Adam, please send one ESU truck. We have a domestic incident. Baby is crying inside the apartment. None of the parents are answering. We need backup. Ten-four."

Minutes later, backup showed up. Two of the police officers held the hundred-pound ram to bust open the door. Upon entering the apartment, what they witnessed was sheer horror.

"Central! Please send an ambulance to Fifty-Five Lauren's Place. We have a severely injured woman. She's also pregnant. And there's a one-year-old baby here. Ten-four."

The neighbor cried, "Melissa!" She looked over at one of the officers. "Is she breathing?"

"Ma'am, you need to step out."

The EMTs arrived. They began to check for vital signs.

"She's going into cardiac arrest! We need to rush her to the hospital right away. She's bleeding profusely and has already lost a lot of blood. The fetal heart rate is extremely low. This woman needs an emergency C-section; otherwise, both her and the baby will not make it," an EMT explained.

A detective arrived on the scene. He began interviewing the neighbor. The detective recorded all of the information concerning the next of kin, beginning with the husband's information. The million-dollar question was, where was Melissa's husband? Locating him became the number-one priority for the police. Melissa was picked up very carefully and placed on a stretcher. She was put into the ambulance and rushed to the nearest hospital.

At the trauma unit in the ER, Melissa was immediately rushed into emergency surgery. The next-door neighbor had called David and Maria to let them know that something awful had happened to Melissa. David and Maria rushed right over to Melissa's building to pick up baby Sarah. The neighbor said she would keep Sarah until they arrived. On the way there, David kept calling Raymond on his cell phone.

"Why isn't he picking up? Where is he when we need him?" David said with frustration. "Raymond, it's David. Please call me as soon as you get this message. Melissa and the baby are in trouble," David said as he left the message on Raymond's voice mail.

When they arrived at the building, Melissa had already been in transport to the hospital. David and Maria, along with baby Sarah, rushed right over to the hospital to find out about Melissa. Almost an hour later, upon arrival, David approached the information desk.

"My daughter, Melissa, she was rushed here. She's nine months pregnant. I'm her father!" David said with his blotchy red eyes.

"Good evening, sir. Hold on," the woman said as she made a phone call.

"Sir, yes, your daughter is upstairs on the fourth floor in the intensive care unit."

"Oh no! Wait! What about her baby? Where's my granddaughter?" David frantically asked.

"She's in the neonatal intensive care unit, sir," the woman explained with a somber look.

While David and Maria anxiously waited in the family room, a doctor entered.

"Hi, I'm Dr. Owens," the doctor said.

"Doctor, how's my daughter?" David desperately asked.

"Your daughter went into cardiac arrest, accompanied by an AFE," the doctor explained.

"Cardiac arrest? What's AFE?" David asked.

"It's an amniotic fluid embolism. The amniotic fluid entered your daughter's bloodstream," the doctor continued to explain. "She's also lost a lot of blood, and although she's been stabilized, she's in a coma." Gasps sounded in the air. "We will have to wait and see what happens within the next forty-eight hours. Your daughter was left for dead," the doctor explained.

"What do you mean?" David shouted.

"I'm so sorry, sir. Your daughter sustained some serious injuries. She has two broken ribs, a broken jaw, and a concussion," the doctor said.

"What? Who could've done this to her?" David asked as the color flushed from his face. He felt a sudden sickening feeling in the pit of his stomach.

David quickly grew faint, and the doctor grabbed him. "Sir, are you okay?" the doctor asked as he helped him to sit down.

Maria sat on a chair, crying.

"What about the baby?" she asked.

"Due to the distress that the baby experienced, there was a lack of oxygen to the baby's brain. The baby is in our neonatal intensive care unit. I'm sorry to inform you, it doesn't look good," the doctor said.

Maria whimpered. "What do you mean?" she asked.

"I'm so sorry, but usually, infants born under these circumstances do not live past forty-eight hours. I'm so sorry to inform you of this, but I just want your family to be prepared. That's all I can tell you at this time," the doctor explained.

Maria released bloodcurdling screams and just cried in David's arms. David continued to call Raymond.

CHAPTER 18

Game Over

> So do not be afraid of them, for there is nothing concealed that will
> not be disclosed, or hidden that will not be made known.
> —Matthew 10:26 (NIV)

RAYMOND HAD BEEN driving erratically on the road back to pick up the truck and the girls. His mind was also racing. How had he lost total control? Did he leave Melissa for dead back at the apartment? Part of him was frightened but mostly for himself. There would be no way out of it this time, once Melissa told someone. Upon arriving at the pharmacy, he found Mike waiting in the front with the two other girls.

"Where have you been?" Mike shouted. "I've been calling you! This truck has to be at the garage right now, and don't forget to drop the girls off first at the club. As soon as you get to the garage, call me," Mike said.

"Okay," Raymond said with a pensive look.

"What's the matter with you?" Mike asked.

"Nothin', nothin'! Oh, I almost forgot. Here's your stuff." Raymond handed a black duffel bag over to Mike.

"Is all the cash still at your place? Your wife doesn't know about the trap, does she?" Mike asked.

"Nah, man, do you think I'm stupid? And yes, all of the cash is still there," Raymond said.

"Hey, watch your mouth? Now get to it. Call me as soon as you drop off the truck. Remember, they're giving you a smaller car to drive back," Mike said.

"Why are we exchanging vehicles again?" Raymond asked.

"Not that it's any of your business, but the truck has all of the stuff in the trunk. And it's gonna take a while to unload and tally up the inventory. No more questions! I'll worry about the details, not you. Got it?" Mike said.

"Okay," Raymond said.

As Raymond began driving, his mind was still frazzled. The girls were in the back smoking.

"Hey! Put that out now! Don't do that while I'm driving!" Raymond yelled at them.

He began driving like a madman. He ran the red light on the corner. Suddenly, a loud siren sounded. Raymond looked in the rearview mirror. The red and blue strobing lights blinded him.

"Girls! Keep your mouths shut! You hear me?" Raymond said loudly as he continued mumbling words of regret under his breath.

It was an unmarked car behind him. It didn't look like a police car, but it had the lights blinking in front. At this point, Raymond assumed that these two men who were approaching the car were cops. They also wore plain clothes.

One guy walked up along the driver's side, where Raymond sat, and the other guy walked along the passenger side while he flashed a light toward the backseat.

The guy on Raymond's side said, "Roll your window down. License and registration." He flashed his gold shield at Raymond.

"Officer, here's my license, but I don't have the registration," Raymond explained.

"Why is that?" the detective asked.

"This isn't my car," Raymond said.

"Who's vehicle is it then?" he asked.

"It's my friend's car," Raymond said.

"What's your friend's name?" the detective asked.

"Mike."

"Mike what?" the detective asked.

"Mike Holmes," Raymond said.

"Who are the girls in the back?" the detective asked.

"Umm, well, they are relatives of my friend. I'm just dropping them off at a party," Raymond said, looking shaken up.

"Wait right here," the detective said as he walked back to his vehicle.

The detective ran a check on the license plate and Raymond's license.

The vehicle had been indeed registered to a Michael Holmes. The detective walked back over to Raymond.

"Do you know that you have a suspended license? There's also a warrant out for your arrest," the detective explained. "Please step out of the vehicle."

"Warrant for my arrest? What did I do?" Raymond asked.

"Step out of the vehicle, sir," the detective said again.

The other detective asked the two girls to step out. He noticed a glassine vial on the floor where they had sat in the back.

"Do you ladies have ID? Let me see them," the other detective asked both girls.

One of the girls had an ID, but the other one didn't. The ID the one girl had looked out of the ordinary.

He asked, "How old are you girls?"

Simultaneously, they both responded, "Eighteen."

The officer who spoke with Raymond asked him to pop open the trunk. Raymond looked like a deer in headlights.

"Sir, I said, pop open the trunk!" the detective ordered loudly.

"Why? You have no grounds to check the trunk. Besides, I told you that this isn't my car," Raymond said angrily.

"Yes, we have the right to check the vehicle. The two girls you have in your car look underage. We suspect the ID is fake. We also found this …" He showed Raymond the empty glassine vial. "Who does this belong to?"

"I don't know. It's not mine," Raymond said.

The two girls shrugged their shoulders as if to suggest that they didn't know either.

"Now pop open the trunk!" the detective said.

Raymond slowly bent down and pressed the button inside of the car to open up the trunk. The other detective walked toward the back.

"Parris! Come back here! It's a body!" the detective yelled.

"Body?" Detective Parris shouted.

Detective Parris handcuffed Raymond and walked over toward the back of the car.

Raymond cried out, "Diamond!"

"You know this woman?" Detective Parris asked.

Raymond put his head down in disbelief, shaking his head.

"Central, this is sector Charlie. We need backup and an ambulance immediately."

"Ten-five, the location?" the radio echoed.

"Location is the corner of First Street and Second Avenue."

"Ten-five, corner of First Street and Second Avenue?"

"Ten-four."

"We have a female; she's breathing but unconscious,"

Detective Parris said as he noticed fresh needle marks on her left arm.

"It wasn't me! You gotta believe me! I didn't know she was back there! She's been missing," Raymond yelped.

In the trunk, they also recovered two kilos of heroin, a bag of Zannies, and oxycodone pills.

"Raymond Perez, you're under arrest," Detective Parris said and began to read him his Miranda rights.

Raymond interrupted. "I didn't kidnap her! I didn't know she was in the car! And the stuff isn't mine! This isn't my car!" Raymond continued to shout.

"Keep it shut!" Detective Parris ordered.

The two young girls who were in the car were trembling and crying. They just kept chanting, "Diamond ... Diamond ..."

The other detective, who detained the young girls, called out, "John! I'm taking the girls back to the precinct!"

"Okay, I'll see you back at the precinct," Detective John Parris said.

Back at the pharmacy, Mike had been making several phone calls. He heard the commotion of police sirens outside. He stepped out and noticed up on the next block, the street had been blocked off with police cars. He began walking a little closer, and he saw his black SUV on the corner where all of the commotion was. From a distance, he caught a glimpse of a man wearing handcuffs. He realized the man was Raymond. Mike turned around and ran back inside of the pharmacy. There was a back exit to the store. He immediately locked up. He ran out and hailed a taxi.

"Going to the Bronx!" Mike said to the driver. "I'll show you how to get there."

After what seemed an eternity, Mike finally arrived in front of Raymond's building in the Bronx.

Upstairs in Raymond's apartment, a police officer stood on an assigned fixed post. It was routine for the police to secure an apartment in which a door had been knocked down. The police officer was standing inside of the kitchen with the window open while he smoked his cigarette.

Mike exited the elevator on the second floor. He saw the door missing. Puzzled, he wondered what had happened. But in sheer desperation, he quickly entered the apartment and ran into Melissa and Raymond's bedroom toward the secret trap inside of the closet. He needed his money, all three hundred thousand dollars.

In the kitchen, the officer heard a sound in the back bedroom.

He approached the bedroom quietly. As he looked in, he tactically approached Mike. He observed him doing something in the closet and heard a mechanical noise. He saw him taking money out.

"Police! Come out of there!" the officer said with his pistol drawn.

Mike got startled. With the money in his hands, he attempted to make a run for it.

"Police! Let me see your hands!" the officer shouted as he ran.

He was able to grab ahold of his shirt. There was quite a struggle between the two. The officer was finally able to subdue Mike after much resistance on his part.

"Get on the ground!" the officer shouted as he quickly placed the handcuffs on him.

The officer patted him down and felt a small wallet in his pocket. He took it out to find his ID. The man he had in custody was Michael Holmes.

"Michael Holmes, you're under arrest!" the officer stated.

"Why am I being arrested? I didn't do nothin'!" Mike shouted.

"Be quiet. You tried to flee after I told you to place your

hands in the air. Then you resisted a police officer," the officer explained. "Do you live here?"

"No, it's my friend's apartment. I came to get something that belongs to me," Mike said.

"Oh yeah? Who's your friend?" the officer asked.

"His name is Raymond. Raymond Perez," Mike said.

"Yeah, well, we are trying to locate your friend. And we're bringing you in for questioning too," the officer said.

"Why?" Mike asked even though he knew Raymond had been arrested.

"Well, we found his pregnant wife severely beaten and left for dead," the officer said.

"What? I had nothing to do with that, man!" Mike shouted with a look of confusion.

"Central, this is sector Adam."

"This is central," the radio echoed.

"Can you raise a patrol supervisor? I'm gonna have one under for resisting, and I need an additional unit for transportation," the police officer stated.

"Ten-five, the location?"

"Location is Fifty-Five Lauren's Place."

"Ten-four, they're en route."

CHAPTER 19

Continued Torment

Though he slay me, yet will I hope in him;
I will surely defend my ways to his face.

—Job 13:15

BACK AT THE hospital in the Bronx, the nightmare of watching their daughter hooked up to a machine with a nest of wires and ventilator was too much for Melissa's parents to bear. The odor of medicine and antiseptic overwhelmed the hospital room. The beeping machine and intravenous drip sounds were perpetual. David and Maria sat beside her bed. Maria had her head down while she prayed out loud. Meanwhile, David stared at Melissa, in his unsettled state of mind. Her face was unrecognizable. It was bandaged up. How had this happened to their only child? David kept blaming himself for not being able to help his daughter. He thought maybe he and Maria should've spent more time around her. Tears just rolled down David's face.

"This isn't your fault, David. It's no one's fault. They just need to find Raymond," Maria said.

"Who could have done this to her? To our family?" David said with grief. "I hope they find him soon. And I don't think I could ever forgive the person who did this," he added discontentedly.

Maria's eyes penetrated him with dread. She reached over and hugged David tightly.

"Maria, I'm going upstairs to the NICU to check on Diana. Will you be okay here?" David asked.

"Yes, you go ahead. We'll take turns switching. I'll go see Diana when you get back," she said somberly. "Pastor Delgado will be here later to pray for our girls."

"Okay, I'll be back," David said and kissed Maria on the top of her head.

Moments later, David just didn't know what to expect. If he thought watching his daughter hanging on by a thread to her life was horrific, nothing could've prepared him for what he was about to see. What should have been a joyous occasion for celebrating instead became his worst nightmare. Baby Diana had oxygen tubes and disc pads with wires connected to them taped all over her tiny chest. She also had a tiny IV and a slew of wires all over. The unit swarmed with the traffic of nurses and doctors coming in and out. A doctor walked in. David approached him.

"Hello, I'm David, baby Diana's grandfather. How is she doing?" David asked.

"We have her stabilized. I'm so sorry for you and your family. I'm sorry to inform you, but she's had substantial damage caused to her brain. She will never be able to speak or walk—" the doctor explained.

David interrupted angrily. "Doctor! Are you saying my granddaughter is in a vegetative state?"

"Well, sir, we never want to put it in those terms, but your granddaughter's life expectancy is anywhere between three and ten days," the doctor said. "I'm so sorry."

"It can't be! There has to be something that you can do! You guys are one of the best! Otherwise, I want a second opinion," David said angrily.

"I understand your frustration. I've been doing this for over twenty years, sir. But I can certainly contact one of the other supervising doctors to come in and speak with you too," the doctor said.

"Yes, I would like to speak to another doctor *now*!" David shouted. Then he broke down, wailing.

"I'll page the other doctor. I'm so sorry. Sir, we have pastoral services here in our hospital. I'll give you their extension," he said.

Suddenly, David's cell phone rang. It was Maria.

"Hi, Maria. Is everything okay?" David said. "Yes. Please send him upstairs to the NICU. We need him right now," he said somberly and hung up.

Within minutes, Pastor Delgado was walking down the hall. David noticed him right away.

"Pastor! Oh thank God you're here!" David wept.

"Hi, David. Maria told me where to find you," Pastor Delgado said as he hugged David.

"Pastor Delgado, the baby ... doctors are giving us about a week or less to say our goodbyes. Please pray with me," David begged.

"Of course, David. You're my family too. This is tragic what has happened to your daughter and grandbaby. Melissa is like a daughter to me too," Pastor Delgado said. "Have they located Raymond?"

"We don't know where he is! He's usually working, and we've been calling him, but he doesn't answer," David said.

Pastor Delgado's face was made up of regret as he let out a big sigh. His eyes welled up.

"David, I feel somewhat responsible. I should've convinced Melissa to stay with you. She just wouldn't do it," Pastor Delgado sadly said.

"What are you talking about?" David asked.

"Melissa, she came to see me recently," he said.

"Oh?" David looked confused. "Well, of course, Pastor. She's been going to the church for years now."

"No, I mean, she came to me for counsel. She told me that Raymond had been hurting her for a long time," Pastor Delgado said regretfully.

"What? That Raymond *what*?" David's faced boiled. Rage filled his eyes. "Raymond has been hurting my daughter?"

"David, calm down. She signed up for weekly counsel and said she would start attending after the birth. She came to me in confidence. Melissa assured me that she would reach out for help after having the baby."

"Oh, my Lord, why?" David said as he looked up to the ceiling, praying. "God! Why my Melissa? Why didn't I know? Raymond!" he shouted.

"David, I understand how upset you are. I already spoke with the police and gave them my statement. I believe in my heart that Raymond did this to Melissa and Diana," Pastor said. "As soon as Maria called me to tell me about her, I called to speak with the detective."

"Give me a minute, Pastor. I'm going to call the detective now. When they find this monster, I want him locked up and the keys thrown away! How could he do this? I treated him like he was my own son!" David snapped.

"David, I completely understand your anger, but—" Pastor Delgado said, but David interrupted.

"I'll be back, Pastor. Have to make this phone call."

As David walked away further down the hall, Pastor Delgado began praying. The situation appeared hopeless. But Pastor Delgado petitioned to God on behalf of David's family. Only a miracle could save baby Diana.

CHAPTER 20

Interrogation

Anyone who does wrong will be repaid for their wrongs, and there is no favoritism.

—Colossians 3:25 (NIV)

THAT NIGHT HAD been just like any other night for Mike. He had been arrested so many times before and always gotten away scot-free. He had the best attorneys in town. This would be just another rap to beat and pay his way out of. He had no clue that this time around, he might be in too deep.

Back in the Manhattan precinct, Raymond was fingerprinted and processed. The detective also entered an "I" card in the system, which was a wanted notification, for Michael Holmes. When his information was entered in their system, it turned out that Michael Holmes had a long rap sheet of sealed records. Detective John Parris then placed Raymond in one of their interrogation rooms.

"Okay. So Raymond Perez, right?"

"Yeah," Raymond replied as he rolled his eyes.

"Where do you live?" Detective Parris asked.

"I live in the Bronx," Raymond said.

"Is your address the same one that's on your license?" he asked.

"Yeah."

"Tell me who Michael Holmes is? And why were you driving his car?" Detective Parris asked.

"I told you, Mike is my friend and I work with him. I was just doing him a favor," Raymond said.

"Oh yeah, doing him a favor transporting drugs and a body in the trunk?" Detective Parris sarcastically asked.

"Nah, man! I had no idea that stuff was back there, especially Diamond. She's my friend," Raymond said.

"Where do you and Mike work?" he asked.

"Mike owns the pharmacy by the Bowery," Raymond said.

"What was your friend Diamond doing in the trunk?" Detective Parris asked.

"I don't know, man! I told you, she was missing. I had no idea of her whereabouts until now, I swear!" Raymond pleaded.

Then there was a knock on the door.

"Detective Parris, we need you a sec," another detective said.

"All right, I'll be right there," Detective Parris said.

Detective Parris turned his attention back to Raymond.

"Mr. Perez. I'll be right back," he said.

"Parris, check it out. One of the guys from the Bronx squad just called. Here's his number. He saw the 'I' card for Michael Holmes in the system. He was arrested in the Bronx for trespassing. They have him in custody right now. Give him a call right away," the detective explained.

"Great! Thanks, man," Detective Parris said.

The phone rang and rang. Someone answered.

"Ah yeah, this is Detective Parris. Can I speak with Detective Diaz?" he asked.

"Sure, hold on," the person said.

Seconds later, he heard, "Detective Diaz here."

"Yeah, hi, I'm Detective Parris. Do you have a Michael Holmes in custody?" he asked.

"Yes, we do. I actually called you. I saw the wanted notification in the system for him. He was in possession of a lot of money, actually three hundred thousand dollars, which he tried to take out of an apartment that was being secured. We also found a pregnant woman who was nearly killed in that same apartment. We suspect he might be responsible, maybe a robbery gone bad," the detective informed him.

"Where is the apartment located?" Detective Parris asked.

"The address is Fifty-Five Lauren's Place, Apartment 2F," Detective Diaz said.

"Wait! What was the address? Did you say Fifty-Five Lauren's Place?" Detective Parris asked, surprised.

"Yeah, why?" he asked.

"Raymond Perez, the man I have in custody, well, that's his residence. Who was the woman found in the apartment?" Detective Parris asked.

"You have Raymond Perez in custody? We've been looking for him. He's the woman's husband," the detective said.

"Is he being transported yet?" Detective Parris asked.

"No, not yet, why?"

"Good. Hold him there. I'm coming over to interrogate him. It sounds like these two guys got something going on," Detective Parris said. "I actually arrested Raymond Perez for possession of drugs, and a young woman was locked in the trunk of Michael Holmes's car," he continued to explain.

"Oh man, really? I'll hold Holmes here for you," Detective Diaz said.

"Thanks, give me about an hour," Detective Parris said.

"Okay, I'll be here. See you soon," Diaz said.

Detective Parris entered the interrogation room.

"Okay, this is what's going on. We found your friend Mike," he said.

Raymond had a surprised look on his face. But he was completely attentive.

Detective Parris continued, "He was arrested for trespassing in your apartment."

Raymond's lips turned white. "What? He was in my apartment?" he said nervously with his eyes wide open.

"Yeah, in your apartment! We think he tried to kill your wife," Detective Parris said.

"Kill my wife? Where is she?"

"She's in the hospital. Now tell me what Mike was doing in your apartment? Why would he want to hurt your wife? Huh?" Detective Parris asked loudly. "If you don't talk to me, you're also gonna get charged for attempted murder on the young girl we found in the trunk of the car you were driving!"

"Listen! I told you! I didn't know she was in the car. I work for Mike at the pharmacy!" Raymond yelled.

"What do you do for him?" Detective Parris asked.

"Well, um, I do a lot of different things. I drive for him, I run his errands, stuff like that," Raymond said.

"You're not really telling me anything. You better talk!" he said.

"Okay, okay. I'll talk about what I know, but what are you gonna do for me?" Raymond asked.

"That all depends on what you tell me. We might be able to help you," Detective Parris said.

"How's Diamond? Is she gonna be okay? Because she can back up what I'm gonna tell you. There is a girl missing who used to work for Mike. Her name is Emily," Raymond said intensely.

"Diamond is in critical condition. But who's Emily? What is her full name?" Detective Parris asked.

"I don't know her full name, but two private investigators came in one day looking for her. Diamond told me that Emily died," he continued to talk as Detective Parris jotted everything down on his pad.

"Do you know the names of those private investigators?" Detective Parris asked.

"Not off the top of my head, but they did leave their cards with me. Their cards are at the pharmacy in Mike's office," Raymond said. "I think they're from Long Island, where the girl's family lives."

"Do you know how she died? Did Mike kill her?" Detective Parris asked.

"No, Diamond said that Emily had an overdose and Mike covered it up. When the private investigators asked him about Emily, he said he'd never seen her before. He also has a drawer filled with a bunch of girls' IDs, fake IDs, and passports too, including Emily's ID. He conducts all of his business out of the pharmacy," Raymond said.

"How many girls work for Mike?"

"I'm not sure, like ten or twelve girls, maybe," Raymond said.

"How old are they?" Detective Parris asked.

"I'm not sure about all of their ages. I know though that Diamond was only sixteen when she started working for Mike, and the girl who died, Emily, was only sixteen too." Raymond kept talking.

"Have you seen other girls at the pharmacy?" Parris asked.

"Yeah, just today. There were three new girls I hadn't seen

before. They looked pretty young. But Mike wouldn't tell me anything about them," Raymond said. "There was a lot he wouldn't tell me. I just drove the girls to and from jobs."

"You saw them there today?" Detective Parris asked.

"Yeah," he answered.

"Okay. There is something that you haven't asked me yet," Detective Parris said.

"What?" Raymond asked, puzzled.

"You just asked me how Diamond was, but before that, I told you that your wife was almost killed and you haven't asked one time how she's doing," Detective Parris said as the thought brought on suspicion.

"Yeah, well, I got a lot on my mind," Raymond said nervously.

"Well, do you know how she is?"

"No, but I will find out," Detective Parris said. "All right. I'll be back." He got up and walked out of the room.

Detective Parris began speaking to the other detective who had been with him when the girl was discovered in the trunk.

"We're gonna need an emergency search warrant for the pharmacy. We need the judge to sign off on this right away. I need you to call the DA with all of the information on the evidence found and have the emergency search warrant drafted. I'm gonna shoot up to the Bronx and interview the guy that they have in custody right now," Detective Parris said in a hurry.

"Got it! I'll write up the report and get this done now," the detective said.

"Thanks! We need to see what's in that pharmacy. And the guy we have now in custody is saying his friend is also responsible for the disappearance of a teen. There could possibly be more girls missing or in trouble," Parris said.

Detective John Parris worked with a special squad within the police department. He used to refer to his squad as the Justice

League. There was one law enforcement officer or agent from a different unit. John worked mostly with narcotics, but his team included agents who also worked crimes associated with immigration, terrorism, human trafficking, and money. They were indeed the justice league. John had been with the detective bureau for twelve years and a police officer for fifteen years in total. This would be the first time he had dealt with a case such as this one. He kept thinking about the pregnant woman who was left for dead. It reminded him of the lovely woman he had met recently at church, where he volunteered. How could anyone hurt a woman in such a way? Even worse than that, how could he hurt a woman carrying a child? John had always wanted to become a police officer to make a difference, to help and save lives. He believed this was what he was meant to do. His mission at that very moment was to solve this case in its entirety.

John arrived at the precinct in the Bronx.

"Hey, how are you doing this evening? I'm here to see Detective Diaz," John said.

"I'm he. Nice to meet you. Come with me," Diaz said. "I'm letting you know now, he's not talking."

"Okay. Is he in here?" John asked.

"Yep, let's go," Detective Diaz said as he walked in with John.

"Michael Holmes?" John asked as he looked at Mike.

"Yeah, you can call me Mike," Mike said.

"Hi, Mike. I'm Detective Parris with the South Manhattan squad. I need to ask you a few questions."

"I already said everything I know," Mike quickly said.

"Okay. Well, do you know Raymond Perez?" John asked.

Mike's demeanor quickly changed. He gave John a serious stare.

"Well? Do you know Raymond Perez?" John asked again.

"I already called my attorney. I'm not speaking anymore to you or anyone," Mike said.

"Okay, if that's the way you want it. You don't have to talk. But I'm gonna tell you this, *Mike*!" John said as his tone got louder. "I have in custody a man named Raymond Perez, who says he works for you. You were caught in his apartment, and his wife's life is hanging by a thread. Your buddy Raymond is singing like a bird. We know about the girl in the trunk of your car, who, by the way, was found alive, Mike. Yes, she's alive. So no problem. We know about the other girls too. We'll see how your attorney is gonna get you outta this one," John said.

"I don't know about no girl in no trunk. And I don't know what girls you're talking about," Mike said.

"Yeah, you don't, huh? Why was a girl locked up in the trunk of your car, Mike?" John shouted.

"I'm waiting to speak to my attorney," Mike said with a snide look on his face.

"Oh, one more thing, as we speak, your pharmacy is in the process of being searched. Now is your opportunity to save yourself and come clean," John said.

Just as John was talking to Mike, his cell phone rang.

"Detective Parris here … Aha, yeah … You got it?... Excellent! … Let me give you a call right back, just finishing up an interview. Give me five minutes."

He turned his sights back to Mike. He said, "Mike, that was one of the detectives from my team. They're searching your place right now!"

"I'm done here, Detective," Mike said.

"No problem! And yes, you are done!" John yelled.

John immediately exited the room. Frustrated, he banged his shield on the desk.

"Diaz, when you're finished drawing up your case and you

speak with the DA, give them all of my information. We need these two cases consolidated. I'll also fax you the details of the search warrant too," John said.

"No problem, Parris, I got you," Detective Diaz said as he shook John's hand. "I'll call you later."

CHAPTER 21

Seek and You Shall Find

The righteous person may have many troubles, but the Lord delivers him from them all.

—Psalm 34:19 (NIV)

DETECTIVE JOHN PARRIS hastened his way to Mike's pharmacy to serve the search warrant. When he arrived, half of the place had been turned upside down. One of the other detectives found something.

"Hey, Parris! Look at this!" the detective exclaimed.

"What is it?" John asked.

"It's a notebook. It looks like they kept a log of everything."

As John skimmed through it, he said, "This is good evidence. It looks like records of all of the money activity. Bag it up."

Downstairs, he heard some yelling. John and two detectives rushed down.

"I found a whole drawer full of IDs!" the detective shouted.

"This is what my subject was talking about," John said as he looked through all of the identifications. He then came across one that caught his eye.

"Emily Johnson," John read out loud.

"Who's Emily Johnson?" the detective asked.

"She's the girl that's been missing. The owner of this place denied even knowing her," John said.

As he continued looking through more of them, he found one that belonged to one of the young ladies who was in the vehicle with Raymond. A look of revulsion was spread all over his face.

The detective asked John, "What's wrong?"

"This girl. She was in the car with my subject. She's only fifteen," John said. "Waiting to hear back from the base, to find out if the two girls are in the missing persons database."

"There's gotta be like a hundred IDs there," the detective said.

"Yeah, and who are all of these young ladies?" John asked.

John continued searching. They pulled shelves and drawers apart and emptied out all closets and cabinets. John noticed a tiny latch behind one of the counters on the wall. It was locked. He took a steel crowbar and smashed it open. When he opened, it appeared to be a secret compartment. He discovered five big black bags within the wall. He opened one, and it contained bundles of money. Inside of the secret compartment, there seemed to be another contraption on the floor. When he pulled it up and opened it, he saw kilos of heroin. There were four square, twelve-by-twelve tan-colored brick-like packages wrapped in what looked like Saran Wrap.

"Back here! I got something!" John shouted for assistance.

With a small flashlight, he searched more to make sure he had everything inside of the compartment, but then, he noticed something. It was on the floor. He flashed his light on the ground. It appeared to be old, dried blood.

"Get the swab kit. I think there's blood on the floor here!" John exclaimed.

After about three hours of searching, John and his team found mounds of evidence in Mike's pharmacy. John requested forensic testing on the blood found on the floor. In total, they found five hundred thousand dollars in cash, three kilos of heroin, and an overflow supply of Zannies, not to mention several girls' IDs, including one of a missing girl. It appeared that John had a solid case against Mike and Raymond as his accomplice. But to seal the deal, he needed to speak with the girl who was discovered in the trunk, Diamond. She would be a strong witness. John also wanted to visit Raymond's wife at the hospital for a possible statement from her or her family.

John's cell phone rang.

"Detective Parris."

"Hey, Parris, I interviewed the girls that were in the car with Perez. After learning their real names and entering their information into the database, it turns out they've been missing. One of them was reported missing six months ago from New Jersey. The other girl was reported missing eight and a half months ago. She's from Upstate New York," the detective explained.

"Oh wow. Let's make sure the families of the girls are located and contacted. We also need statements from them," John said. "We're wrapping everything up here. I'll see you in a few."

The Next Day

"Parris, what's on your agenda today?" a detective asked John.

"I'm on my way out to go to the hospital," John said.

"The hospital?" the detective asked.

"Yeah, I want to interview the wife of the guy I arrested last night. I need to know the details of what happened the night of her attack," John said.

"Yeah, I heard about that. I heard she was beaten pretty bad. And she was pregnant too," the other detective said as he shook his head.

"I want these guys put away for a long time," John said.

"I hear ya. I'll see you later," the detective responded.

Upon arrival at the hospital, John approached the information desk and flashed his gold badge.

"Good morning, I'm Detective John Parris. I'm here to find out about a pregnant woman who has been severely beaten. She was rushed in here last night. I'm one of the investigating detectives," he explained.

"Good morning, Detective. Let me call upstairs and see what I can do," the front desk clerk said as she picked up the phone to call.

While John waited, he heard someone call for him.

"John?"

"Pastor Delgado! How are you? What are you doing here?" John asked, surprised.

"I'm here visiting a friend and member of our church. As a matter of fact, you met this young lady," Pastor Delgado said.

"Oh really? Who? And what happened?" John asked.

"Do you remember the lovely woman, the one you met at the church, who was pregnant? Her name is Melissa. The day you needed my help and you asked for her advice on the artwork?" Pastor Delgado asked.

"Oh, right! Yes! Melissa! I guess she gave birth earlier than she expected, huh?" John asked.

"Oh no, John. Something terrible has happened to her and her baby. She was found by the police unconscious in her apartment from a severe attack," Pastor Delgado explained.

"Oh no! What?" John looked confused. "Wait … Pastor,

does her husband happen to be Raymond Perez?" John asked, looking disturbed.

"Yes. Raymond Perez is her husband," Pastor Delgado answered. "Why? Do you know him?"

"I arrested that guy last night. Another man who's associated with him was also arrested. He was in their apartment stealing money," John said with a flushed look.

"Raymond was arrested? Oh my word," Pastor Delgado said. "What for?"

"It's too much to get into. It's just not good," John said with hesitation. He had a somber, pensive look on his face.

"How could anyone hurt such a precious person as Melissa?" John asked. "Can I go see her now?"

"I just came down to buy a cup of coffee. But I'll certainly take you to see her. By the way, John, what are you doing here? Letting the family know about Raymond?" Pastor Delgado asked.

"So weird, Pastor, I actually came here investigating this case. I came to interview her or the family, but I didn't know that the woman I was coming to interview was Melissa," John said. "What a small world."

"Oh, I almost forgot, you can probably speak to her family, but Melissa is in a coma," Pastor Delgado said regretfully.

"She's in a coma?" John asked. "What did he do to her?"

"She sustained a broken jaw, broken ribs, and a concussion. Her face is gravely swollen. The doctors also just discovered swelling in her brain as well. John, do the police know who did this to her?" Pastor Delgado asked.

"We're not sure, but we suspect Raymond's associate had something to do with it," John explained. "Why, Pastor?"

"Well, I gave my statement to the police. The day you met Melissa, she told me that Raymond had been physically abusive toward her for years. That's why I was wondering," Pastor Delgado said.

"He has? Oh man. No wonder!" John exclaimed.

"No wonder what?" Pastor Delgado asked.

"It's a lot, Pastor. Can you please just take me to see her family? And what about her baby?"

"Oh, John. The baby is in critical condition. Doctors gave the family about a week to make preparations," he said.

"Oh, dear Lord, save the innocent baby, and save Melissa," John said as he began to pray out loud worriedly. "Why do bad things happen to good people?"

"Come on, John. Let's go upstairs," Pastor Delgado said.

CHAPTER 22

More Bad News

> What strength do I have, that I should still hope? What prospects, that I should be patient? Do I have the strength of stone? Is my flesh bronze? Do I have any power to help myself, now that success has been driven from me?
>
> —Job 6:11–13 (NIV)

DAVID SAT IN the room where Melissa lay. Maria went to be with baby Diana in the NICU. Little Sarah was staying with Maria's sister. He continued reading scriptures out loud from his Bible. It became a more discouraging day for the family when they received news of the swelling in Melissa's brain that morning. It wasn't looking good. Baby Diana's condition had also continued to be critical. The doctors confirmed that the family needed to start preparing themselves and make the necessary arrangements. There could be nothing done to change the inevitable.

"Oh, Melissa, I know you can hear me, honey. It's Daddy. Remember when you were in kindergarten and you came to me one day because you wanted to learn how to ride a bike? I thought about how cute and little you were. I was so proud at how courageous and determined you were. You even asked me to learn without the training wheels. Most kids at that age at first could be intimidated by just the thought of riding a bike, but not you. You are still my courageous, strong girl. Sarah and Diana need you, sweetheart. Mom and I love you. We need you too. I know you have a long life ahead of you. Please come back to us," David said to her.

Suddenly, the heart monitor sped up.

Immediately, a loud noise sounded. Nurses and doctors rushed in.

"I'm sorry, sir. You need to step out!" one of the nurses said.

"What's happening to her?" David exclaimed.

"Sir, we really need you to step out."

As David walked out, the door slammed behind him. He could see through the small glass window in the door that Melissa was in trouble.

"David!" someone called him. It was the pastor.

"Pastor Delgado, something is wrong with Melissa!" David yelled in panic.

"What's the matter?" Pastor Delgado asked.

"I don't know. I began talking to her, and all of a sudden, the heart monitor just went off. I think she might've heard me," David said as he looked at the man standing next to the pastor.

"David, this is John. John, this is David, Melissa's father," Pastor Delgado introduced them to each other, and they shook hands.

"Nice to meet you," David said with curiosity. "What brings you here?"

Pastor Delgado interrupted. "Well, David, this is going to sound strange, but John here is a detective with the New York Police Department."

"Okay?" David said as he waited to hear more.

"Well, he came here to give you information about Raymond," Pastor Delgado explained.

Abruptly, a doctor came out of Melissa's room. His face was filled with gloom.

"What!" David yelled.

"I'm sorry, sir. Your daughter's heart rhythm became chaotic, which was probably preventing blood being pumped to her heart, but—"

"No! Please tell me no!" David interrupted as he shouted again.

"We had to perform a cardiac defibrillation and were able to stabilize her heart. But we had to induce her back into a coma," the doctor explained.

"Why? And what is a cardiac defibrillation?" David frowned.

"It's an emergency procedure that administers an electric shock to the heart using a defibrillator. And if we didn't induce her into a coma, her heart could've gone into shock, and she might have eventually suffered a fatal heart attack," the doctor said.

"Lord, why my Melissa? Where are You?" David cried as he looked up. He was once again anguished with the dreadful news.

"I'll stay here and pray with you," John said.

"Thank you, John," David said with watery eyes. "So, you're here about Raymond?"

"Oh yeah. I actually came here to interview Melissa or her family. I also recently met your daughter through Pastor Delgado, but I had no idea that she was Raymond's wife," John explained.

David looked at him kind of confused. He asked, "So how do you know Raymond?"

"Well, that's just it; like Pastor told you, I'm a detective with the NYPD. I actually arrested Raymond last night," John said.

"Arrested Raymond? Oh my word! What for now?" David cried out.

"It's a long story, David. But let's just say it's bad news. Your son-in-law could be facing a lot of prison time for possession of illegal drugs, possible homicide, and kidnapping of minors," John said regretfully.

"Oh no! What are you talking about 'possible homicide'?" David asked.

"I'm so sorry, David. Raymond might be involved with the disappearance of a girl who allegedly is now deceased. There are a lot of convoluted details involved. But before I get into any of that, how was Raymond's relationship with your daughter?" John asked.

"It's complicated. I just learned that Raymond had been abusive toward my daughter. I always thought things were okay between them until a few months ago when my son-in-law got in trouble with the law. Melissa also told me that they were having some problems, but she never really told me about what. I just figured it was the normal stuff that husbands and wives go through," David said.

"We're trying to determine what happened in your daughter's apartment the night she was attacked. A man was caught in there stealing money from them. Investigators found a strange-looking secret compartment in the wall of your daughter's bedroom," John said.

"Huh, secret compartment? That's odd. My daughter didn't have a secret compartment in her bedroom." David scowled.

"It was built inside of the walk-in closet located in their bedroom," John continued.

"Wait a minute!" David exclaimed. "Yes! Melissa was so happy about that closet. Raymond arranged for her and the baby to stay with us for about four or five days because he hired a contractor to renovate their apartment. He surprised her with the new closet," David said.

"Really?" John said as he jotted something down on his small notepad. "When was this, recently?"

"Yes, it was just a couple of weeks ago," David said. "My daughter definitely wasn't aware of a secret compartment. That good for nothing! That had to be Raymond!" David sneered.

"I know this is going to be difficult for you to hear, but we believe the man who's associated with your son-in-law attacked Melissa. And we're trying to find out why," John said. "Was it a robbery gone bad, and he came back to steal the money? Or did Raymond hire him? We need to find out the facts."

"How could I be so stupid?" David said. "I worked as a detective myself and did police work for twenty-six years. How did I not see all of the signs? I let Melissa down," David said.

"None of this is your fault. I've seen this type of situation so many times before," John consoled him. "I have a lot of work to do. I'm going to find out who did this to her. But can I stay here with you for a while?" John asked.

"With all due respect, Detective, can't you see my daughter is in a coma? Wasn't interviewing me enough?" David asked.

"Oh, David, it's not what you think. Even though I only met your daughter once, I felt like I knew her for years. She belongs to the same church as me. At this point, I'd just like to stay and pray with you, but only if you're okay with that. If not, I totally understand," John said.

David looked at him as if he couldn't believe what he had just said to him.

"Sure you can. We could use a lot of prayer right now," David said.

CHAPTER 23

Truth

> Have nothing to do with the fruitless deeds of darkness, but rather expose them. It is shameful even to mention what the disobedient do in secret.
>
> —Ephesians 5:11–12

DAVID PACED INTENSELY back and forth in the hospital's family room. He felt uneasy. His grief over his daughter and granddaughter turned into motivation for helping to solve this case. A light bulb went off in his head. David personally knew the superintendent of the building where Melissa resided. He remembered something that could maybe help in this case.

Meanwhile, Melissa remained in a coma, and baby Diana clung to life. Being a retired police officer, David still had a lot of resources and connections with those who were in the police department. But this case now involved his only daughter. He took it upon himself to start his own investigation.

"Hey, Vince. It's David," he said while speaking on the phone.

"Hi, Dave. How's it going? I'm sorry to hear about Mel and the baby," the superintendent said.

"Listen, you and I've known each other a long time, right?" David said.

"Yeah, of course," Vince said.

"I need a huge favor from you," David said.

"Anything for you, man."

"I know the police are doing their investigation, but this is now involving my own flesh and blood. How far back does your surveillance footage go? Do you think you can take me to your surveillance room?" David asked.

"It rotates about every four to five months. Why? How far back do you need to see?" Vince asked.

"That's good news. I need to see the footage from like two weeks ago. Any chance you can make that happen?" David asked.

"Absolutely, Dave. When do you want to come in? I'm here now," he said.

"Great. Give me about ten minutes," David said.

"In fact, I'll give you the room for as long as you need it or until you find what you're looking for. You know I wouldn't do this for anybody else," Vince said.

"Thanks, Vince. I owe you big-time," David said gratefully.

"You don't owe me anything. Whatever I can do to be of help to you and your family. This is the least I can do," Vince said.

"I'll see you in a few," David said, hurried.

About an Hour Later

When David finally arrived at the building where Melissa lived, he immediately went to see the super.

"Vince, I'll never forget this," he said.

"Don't worry about it. Like I told you before, take as much

time as you need. I'll be upstairs. If you need anything else, call me," Vince said.

"I brought my flash drive. I am going to download any footage I may need. Is that okay?" David asked.

"Sure, Dave, no problem."

"I'll call you when I'm done," David said.

"Okay."

The surveillance camera system was quite simple for David to navigate. He had entered the dates that Melissa and Sarah had stayed with them, the time Raymond was renovating their apartment. He pressed play and began to watch. At first, it didn't appear like much was going on. He recognized the college student who lived next door to Melissa walking out in a hurry. Then he noticed the little old couple who lived one floor below Melissa walking into the building with groceries. It was a multicamera system, so there was a lot to observe, but nothing seemed out of the ordinary until he finally noticed Raymond walking with another man. He'd never seen this man before. Moments later, he watched that same man walk out of the building alone, and within minutes, he saw him again; only this time, he returned with a few other guys. He quickly turned his attention to camera number 11, which was the surveillance camera on Melissa's floor.

David continued to watch as the men exited the elevator and eventually entered the apartment. He thought maybe this was just the crew that Raymond hired to help renovate the apartment. But that idea quickly vanished when he saw the men carrying in long tables, duffel bags, and other materials. They also didn't look like construction workers. They looked more like a bunch of street thugs.

David didn't want to jump to conclusions, but his gut kept gnawing at him. He continued watching. He saw the man who had walked into the building with Raymond that first day a

lot. As he continued to watch, something just didn't seem right
to him. When Raymond had done the renovations, the floors
were sanded throughout the whole apartment, but David did
not see the sanding machine brought into the building until the
fourth day that the crew was there. Then he saw the main guy
finally carrying in the sanding machine. On the fourth day, he
also noticed wood building materials that he carried, similar to
materials used for making the closet. What had they been doing
for the first three days before that? He also noticed on the third
day, the tables were carried out. David saved all of the footage.

Next, he entered the date of Melissa's attack. He began to
watch from the early morning hours of that date he entered.
David fast-forwarded the footage throughout that day. Not much
appeared unusual. Suddenly, David slowed down the footage.
It was Raymond. He watched as he stormed into the building,
walked into the elevator, and then exited the elevator and opened
the door to the apartment. Nearly an hour later on the footage,
he watched as Raymond stormed out of the apartment, carrying
a black duffel bag with some kind of white sporting goods logo
on it. When Raymond entered the elevator, David zoomed in
on camera number 3, which was the surveillance camera inside
of the elevator. He kept his eyes on the screen and watched
Raymond fidget and search through his pockets. He pulled out a
small handkerchief while he scrubbed his hands hard. It looked
like blood. Then, he watched Raymond quickly exit the elevator
and run out of the building. David's intuition kicked in. He fast-
forwarded again. What he then saw made him sick to his stomach.
He watched as the neighbor frantically banged on Melissa's door
and then pulled out her cell phone. He fast-forwarded more.

Two police officers arrived, entered the building, and got
into the elevator. And there it was, on camera 11, the same two
police officers on Melissa's floor. David watched the next-door

neighbor. She was clearly distraught. He fast-forwarded more, and then another crew of police officers arrived and broke down the door. David paused the footage. His heart pounded in his chest. After he regained his composure, he pressed play again. He continued to watch the disturbing images of cops and the EMTs going in and out of Melissa and Raymond's apartment. There it was, the image of his daughter laid out on a stretcher. Baby Sarah cried while the neighbor held her in her arms. After watching all of the unsettling footage of commotion, he fast-forwarded. He noticed a cop enter the apartment. Not too long after, David saw something else. He watched a man enter the building. The man looked familiar. It then materialized in his mind that this was the same man who had been with Raymond on the previous footage from the week Melissa had stayed with them. Why was he there? He must have been the guy the police had caught stealing. There was one of his questions answered. Raymond had actually been the last person with Melissa. He realized then it had to be Raymond who had attacked his daughter. David grabbed his cell phone out of his back pocket and began dialing.

The phone rang.

"Hello? John?"

"Hey, David. How's it going?" John answered.

"I need to come by your office today. I have something important to give to you that'll help with your case," David said.

"Whatcha got?" John asked.

"I got footage from the surveillance camera system in my daughter's building," he said.

"What? David, let us take care of that. We're on top of it. I don't want you worried about this. I promised you that I would find the person who hurt Melissa," John said. "Besides, your family needs you right now."

"Well, John, this is the best way I know, at this point, to help my family. And, by the way, I already found out who hurt my daughter. When can I meet you? I want this piece of work put away for a long time," David said.

"Who?" John asked.

"Raymond! I want him put away for good. He hurt my baby!" he exclaimed. "There's a lot of footage I need you to see."

"Give me about an hour. I'll call you to let you know where to meet?" John said.

Back at the Hospital

Maria sat right beside Melissa. From the way that she looked, it appeared to her as if Melissa had little chance of ever recovering. There she lay, looking sound asleep but surrounded by a blend of humming and beeping noises. She continued to speak to Melissa about baby Sarah while holding her hand. She spoke of how much Sarah missed her mama. After endless hours of watching Melissa, as she was about to get up from the chair, unexpectedly, she felt her hand twitch.

"Melissa, can you hear me?" Maria was startled. "Melissa?"

And then, there was another twitch. Maria gently squeezed her hand. Suddenly, Melissa instantaneously and gently squeezed back.

"Oh my goodness! Melissa? Baby, it's Mom. I'm right here with you," Maria said desperately.

Melissa's eyes opened slightly. She could see the cloudy, blurring shape of someone looking at her. Maria's voice echoed in Melissa's ears. The sounds around her resonated far away. But then her eyes suddenly fell shut again.

"Nurse! Hurry! She's awake!" Maria yelled out while pressing the button for assistance. "Nurse!" Maria continued to shout.

One of the nurses finally walked in.

"What's wrong?" she asked.

"My daughter! She squeezed my hand and opened her eyes," Maria vehemently said.

The nurse examined her. Her vital signs were stable. She noticed Melissa's eyes were closed.

"Are you sure that she opened her eyes?" she asked.

"I'm positive! Her eyes opened up a little, and she squeezed my hand too," Maria said.

"Okay, ma'am. Let me locate the doctor," the nurse said.

CHAPTER 24

Fallen

And have you completely forgotten this word of encouragement
that addresses you as a father addresses his son? It says, "My son,
do not make light of the Lord's discipline, and do not lose heart
when he rebukes you, because the Lord disciplines the one he loves,
and he chastens everyone he accepts as his son. Endure hardship as
discipline; God is treating you as his children. For what children are
not disciplined by their father?"

—Hebrews 12:5–7 (NIV)

Later that Afternoon

DAVID FINALLY MET with John. He was grateful for David's involvement in helping with his case. It had also been clear to him, after a few hours of viewing the surveillance footage, that Raymond was indeed responsible for Melissa's and infant Diana's attacks. Melissa's bloody clothing had also been swabbed for DNA testing. In addition to the list of crimes Raymond had been charged with, they were also going to add the charge of three counts of attempted murder.

Raymond's Arraignment

The clerk of the court said, "All rise! Honorable Judge Matthew McNally is in court."

The judge said, "Court is now in session. Call the cases."

The clerk of the court read, "In the matter of the *People of the State of New York versus Raymond Perez,* Counsel, please state your appearances."

The prosecuting attorney said, "Your Honor, I am Attorney Patricia Abrams."

"Your Honor, I'm Attorney Jacob Dansky," said the defense attorney.

Judge McNally said, "Mr. Raymond Perez, if at any time during these proceedings anything confuses you or you do not understand, please interrupt me so that your attorney can explain it to you. Ms. Abrams, will you please state the charges that have been made against Mr. Perez in this case."

"In the State of New York, within the jurisdiction of this honorable court, Mr. Raymond Perez has been charged with three counts of attempted murder in the second degree, assault and battery in the first degree, criminal possession of controlled substances with the intent to sell, kidnapping of a minor, running a child prostitution ring, and money laundering."

"I understand that Mr. Perez is planning to plead not guilty to the charges brought by the people," the judge said. "I must make sure that you understand your statutory and constitutional rights before I take your plea. You have a right to be represented by counsel at this arraignment. If you cannot afford an attorney, one will be appointed to you by the state. Have you retained counsel in this matter?"

Raymond replied, "Yes, Your Honor."

"You have the right to a hearing within ten days after the entry of a plea. You have the right to a speedy trial, but your case must be brought to trial within forty-five days of this arraignment. You have a right to waive this right, in which case, the court will set a trial date. You have a right to a trial by jury. At your trial, you have the right to have witnesses to testify on your behalf. You have the right to remain silent, which also means you cannot be forced to take the witness stand. You have a right to a preliminary hearing to determine probable cause that a felony has indeed been committed and that you are the person who committed these crimes. At the hearing, you have the same rights I have just explained to you today. Do you understand your rights?"

Raymond answered, "Yes, Your Honor."

"Do you have any questions about what you are doing here today, before you enter your plea?"

"No, Your Honor."

"Mr. Dansky, do you think that you've had sufficient time to discuss this case with your client? Have you explained the defenses, rights, and possible outcomes of his plea with him? And are you content that your client understands these things?"

"Yes, Your Honor."

"Mr. Perez, are you ready to enter your plea?"

"Yes, I am, Your Honor."

"To the charges mentioned at the beginning of these proceedings, what is your plea?"

"Not guilty, Your Honor."

"This court finds that the plea was voluntarily made with the understanding of the nature of the charges, in addition to the consequences of the plea. This court accepts the defendant's plea of not guilty. We will now set a date for the preliminary hearing within the next ten days."

Back at the Hospital

David returned to the hospital.

"How's my grandbaby doing?" David asked.

"She is definitely a fighter. She is a living, breathing miracle. We are doing all we can, sir, but the survival rate for an infant in her condition is very little to none."

David remained quiet as he prayed to himself. Maria remained in the ICU with Melissa. David's cell phone began ringing. He scurried out of the NICU to answer the call.

"Hey, John, what's going on?"

"David, I just wanted to let you know that Raymond's arraignment was earlier."

"Okay. How'd it go?" David asked.

"He pleaded not guilty," John said hesitantly.

"What?" David shouted and then tried to compose himself. A nurse passing by looked at him kind of startled.

"I know. I know. Don't worry. The judge didn't set bail for him. He's staying right in there," John assured him.

"What about the other guy?" David asked.

"Oh, you mean Raymond's partner? Yes, his arraignment was this morning. He also pleaded not guilty. The judge didn't set bail for him either. They're both considered flight risks," John explained.

"Now what?" David asked.

"Now, we get to work building this case. I want justice for Melissa and her baby. I want justice for those young girls that they were taking advantage of too."

"What about the missing girl? Any word on her?" David asked.

"No, not yet, but we also sent everything out for forensic testing," John said. "Is it okay if I stop by later to come visit Melissa?" John asked.

"Sure, no problem."

Prison near Manhattan Island

"Holmes, you have a phone call," the correctional officer shouted.

Mike walked down the dingy hallway in handcuffs, while the other inmates howled and shouted.

"There he goes! Mikey always gets away with it!" an inmate shouted.

"You got one minute!" the correctional officer said loudly.

Mike gave him a stone-faced look. He grabbed the phone. "Hello? ... Uh-huh? ... Okay? ... Really? ... Yesss! Thanks, man! This is why I pay you the big money. Okay, I'll see you soon." Mike gloated with a wide smile on his face, as he had just received the best news from his attorney.

The correctional officer quickly handcuffed him and began walking him back to his cell. Mike continued to laugh to himself.

"I told all of ya that I am untouchable. You all just wasting taxpayers' money putting me in here. I'm outta here," Mike boasted.

"Yeah, yeah. Keep talking. You ain't out just yet," the correctional officer stated.

About an Hour Later

It was mealtime for the inmates. Mike sat at the usual table with a couple of the other inmates who were familiar to him. Mike was in his glory.

"Man, I tell you. The system can never beat me. They got nothin' on me. And everything is all hearsay," Mike arrogantly boasted.

"Oh yeah? Why is that, Mikey?" one of the inmates asked.

"My lawyer got bail for me. I'll be outta here in the next couple of hours. I'm invincible, bro. Money talks. And as long as I got plenty of it, nobody can touch me. This case against me is gonna be dropped; you'll see," Mike continued to praise himself. "They got nothin'!"

"Well, you think you're so untouchable, Mikey. Do you know what I'm in for?" an inmate asked.

"Nah, man, and honestly, I don't really care." Mike smirked.

"Mikey, they call me a killa, the grim reaper; they call me the hit man."

Mike suddenly felt a burning, throbbing sensation in his back. He slowly reached behind to touch it and brought his hand back up to look. Mike had no idea what had just happened. Immediately, he looked over and felt a cold chill around his neck. He began choking, while holding his neck with both hands. It happened all too quickly. Mike dropped to the ground face-first, but no one helped him. Alarm bells began piercing. Everyone spread out and away from him. Correctional officers rushed in shouting. But all of the inmates claimed that they saw nothing. No eyewitnesses came forward to describe Mike's attack.

Manhattan Precinct

John's phone hadn't stopped ringing in the last couple of days with his latest case.

"Detective Parris here."

"We have a problem," the detective on the other line said.

"What's up?" John asked.

"It's about Michael Holmes," he said.

"Yeah, what about him?"

"Well, he was just killed in prison," the detective said.

"What? Killed? How?" John gasped.

"He was shanked in the back and throat. He died right away. No one is saying who actually did it." The detective continued to explain, "One of the confidential informants finally came forward to cut some of his time off. He claimed it was an ordered hit."

"A hit? By who?" John asked.

"Well, the girl you found in the trunk, her father is doing time in federal prison upstate. Supposedly, he saw the news about her and had a hit put on him."

"Father? But when interviewing Raymond, he said that she was abandoned by her parents," John said, puzzled.

"Let's get someone out there to interview the father. In the meantime, this changes everything. We requested to have these two cases merged together. The girl, Diamond—actually her real name is Donna—agreed to testify against this guy. Thank God she is stable now and is going to make it. In an interview, she told my partner that Michael Holmes actually murdered the missing girl Emily. She was afraid to tell anyone the version of what really happened before. Emily had confided in Donna, telling her that Mike abused her all of the time. Now, obviously there is no case against Holmes. We still got a lot of evidence against Raymond Perez," John said. "Let's get to work."

CHAPTER 25

It is Finished

For you created my inmost being; you knit me together in my mother's womb. I praise you because I am fearfully and wonderfully made; your works are wonderful, I know that full well. My frame was not hidden from you when I was made in the secret place, when I was woven together in the depths of the earth. Your eyes saw my unformed body; all the days ordained for me were written in your book before one of them came to be.

—Psalm 139:13–16

PASTOR DELGADO WAS thankful he had associate pastors to cover for him at the church, as he had not left the hospital. He continued praying over Melissa and baby Diana.

"Pastor, thank you so much for everything. It means a lot to our family," Maria said.

"Of course. Melissa is like a daughter to me. She also understood the power of prayer. I have no doubt in my mind that she's hearing every single word of truth that we speak over her."

Unexpectedly, Melissa's eyes appeared to be rolling under her eyelids. It looked like her mind was fighting.

"Melissa? It's Mom. Can you hear me?"

Melissa's hand twitched, and her eyes continued to move while closed. Suddenly …

"Diana!" Melissa cried out as she abruptly opened her eyes as if she had just awoken from a nightmare.

"No, it's me, Mom," Maria reassured her.

"Mom?"

"Oh my goodness, Melissa!" Maria exclaimed and reached over to hug her.

"Pastor Delgado?" Melissa looked over at him.

"Yes, sweetheart, I'm here," Pastor Delgado said.

"Where is Sarah? And where's my baby, Diana. I want to see her. Is she okay?" Melissa desperately kept asking.

She tried to sit up but didn't have the strength.

"How long have I been asleep? Where's Diana? I need to see her," Melissa pleaded.

"Sweetheart, Diana is in the NICU," Maria said with a dreadful look in her eyes.

"Mom, what's wrong with her? I know that look!"

"You need to gather your strength, love."

"No, Mom, I want to go see her now," Melissa demanded.

"Okay, let me get the doctor and see what he says."

After the doctor's approval and removal of her facial bandages, Melissa was going to be able to see Diana. She refused to eat anything. Her main focus was on getting up and going to see her baby.

"Honey, I called your dad and the nice detective on your case," Maria said.

"Detective? What detective?" Melissa was baffled.

"Your friend, love."

"My friend? I don't have any detective friends, Mom."

"Yes, his name is John. He said he attends the same church."

"John?" Melissa still looked confused.

Pastor Delgado joined in the conversation.

"Yes, Melissa. Do you remember the day you came in for counsel and you met a gentleman?" he reminded her.

"Ohhhh yes. John. Wait … I didn't know he was a cop."

"Yes, sweetheart, it's a long story, honey. He is also the one who arrested Raymond. Apparently, he's in serious trouble. Not to mention, we know he did this to you and Diana," Maria said.

"Yes, Mom. He tried to kill me. I pray to God that he will be put away forever. I will never forgive him for this one. Mom, I'm sorry to say this, but I feel nothing but hate in my heart for him," Melissa said.

"Sweetheart, I know this is a difficult time. You don't mean what you're saying right now."

Melissa quickly interrupted. "Oh, I know exactly what I'm saying. He hit me for years. He broke me down. I never want to see him ever again," she said bitterly.

"Are you ready to go see Diana?" Maria asked.

"Yes."

Moments later, she entered the NICU. Although not in good shape at all, Melissa whisked her way down the hall.

"Where's Diana?" she asked.

A doctor met her eyes.

"Nice to meet you, Mrs. Perez," the doctor greeted Melissa.

"Hello, Doctor. How's my baby?" Melissa looked fearful.

"Ah, okay. I'm guessing they haven't told you," the doctor said as he looked over at Maria and Pastor Delgado.

"Told me what?" Melissa asked excitedly.

Maria walked closer to Melissa and began holding her.

"I'm actually glad to see you're doing better and able to come see her. We informed your family that your daughter sustained a substantial brain injury. We don't really know exactly how much time she has left," the doctor regretfully explained.

"What! *Nooo!*" Melissa kept screaming and crying as she fell to her knees. "No, not her. My God! What are You doing? Where are You?" Melissa sobbed and loudly spoke out while looking up to the ceiling.

"Why?" She kept crying.

Maria bent down and crouched over her to console her.

"I'm so sorry," the doctor said to Melissa.

"Take me! Take me, Lord! Not her." Melissa was inconsolable.

Pastor Delgado put his hand on her and prayed.

After some time of her mother and pastor trying to calm her down, Melissa suddenly became still. She swallowed hard and asked, "Can I go inside to see her? I just want her to hear my voice."

Melissa was allowed to go in and say her goodbyes. She walked in to see her newborn baby attached to several wires. She lay inside of what looked like an incubator. It had a little window that could open and close. Baby Diana's skin was a pale-clay color. Melissa sat in a chair right beside her. With tears rolling down her face, she put her hand against the window and began to pray, "Lord, I know that You didn't bring me and Diana through all of this to just let her die. Lord, in Isaiah 49:15 (NIV), Your word says, 'Can a mother forget the baby at her breast and have no compassion on the child she has born? Though she may forget, I will not forget you!' I know that You have my child in mind and will not forget her. I know that she is long lived and durable. Lord, in Psalm 139, it states that You knitted her together in my womb. I know that my baby is fearfully and wonderfully made. Diana is my gift. I promise to treasure and love the gifts given to me by You. I thank you that no weapon formed against her innocent life will prosper. In Jesus's name. Amen."

The Next Day at the Prison

Word of Mike's murder spread like wildfire in the prison. But it was just another day for most. In fact, word had it that most were happy about it. He was a familiar face they had seen around, but he never got pinned for anything. Time was up for good ole Mike.

Raymond just got word about Mike. His attorney advised him to change his plea to guilty and to talk; otherwise, prosecutors planned on pinning Mike's crimes on him as well. No matter what, it didn't look good for Raymond.

Raymond sat out in the yard where most of the inmates played basketball or had some kind of exercise. He was pensive. An inmate walked up to him, one he'd seen before. The guy was an older man, well-built, and had a large, intricate tattoo of skulls on his left forearm. His salt-and-pepper hair and well-groomed goatee made him stand out from the others. The majority of the other inmates were younger.

"What's up, bro?" The inmate grinned at Raymond.

"Hey," Raymond responded in a monotonic voice.

"You look like you just lost your best friend or something."

"Yeah, man, my boy, Mike, got killed yesterday. I got a lot on my mind. Looks like I might have to make a deal with the prosecutors," Raymond said.

"Deal? What kind of deal? Don't tell me you're a rat?" the inmate said in a snide tone.

"Nah, man, nothing like that. I'm just not going down for something I didn't do. Imma take it like a man and fess up to my own crimes," Raymond explained.

"Ah, that's it. Take it like a man. You know what I'm in for?" the inmate asked with a smile on his face.

"Nah, man, I don't."

"Well, they call me a killa, the grim reaper; they call me the go-to guy to take another brother out."

Raymond looked at him, kind of confused.

"Oh, and by the way, Donna's father said to tell you hello," the inmate said sarcastically.

Instantaneously, one, two, three, four ... ten seconds with ten swift deep jabs of pressure Raymond felt in his stomach and the inmate disappeared in a flash, just like that. Raymond lay on the floor. His mind raced with blurry images of Melissa and then of Sarah; his heart rate rapidly dropped and then all went black.

EPILOGUE

Forget the former things; do not dwell on the past.
See, I am doing a new thing! Now it springs up; do you not perceive it?
I am making a way in the wilderness and streams in the wasteland.
—Isaiah 43:18–19 (NIV)

Seven Years Later

IT WAS THE hottest day in July. The baby-blue sky lit up with a sunburst of bright light. There was not a cloud in the sky. Pastor slowly walked, while using his cane for support, into a room full of young men who had lost their way, a group of men needing some spiritual guidance and advice. The young men were a diverse group from just about every culture, color, and race. Some looked eager to hear what Pastor had to say. Others didn't look so enthusiastic.

"Hello. I'm very honored and excited to be here to talk with you all today. You must be asking yourselves, 'Why would a pastor even waste his time to talk with me?' Maybe some of you are not religious at all. And that's okay. My talk with you today, gentleman, is not about religion at all. First, I'm here to tell you a little bit about myself. But I'm also here to tell you how Jesus

Christ saved my life. He doesn't discriminate. He's not concerned about religion. He doesn't care about what you've done in your past or how bad you were. It doesn't matter where you came from, if you're rich or poor. It doesn't even matter to Him if you've ever even believed in Him or not. He's always there with us every second of every day, waiting for the chance to show you His mercy and love. You see, gentlemen, my name is Pastor Raymond Perez, and I'm an inmate at another prison in Upstate New York. I was just like you are. I grew up as an only child with a single mother. I never knew my dad. But I did have a lot of quote unquote *uncles*, men who beat me and told me that I was a no-good runt. My mom believed in God, but growing up, I never did. I always thought if there was a God, why would He allow me to live a childhood filled with suffering. You see, gentlemen, the devil is a liar and the accuser of the brethren. I grew up living a lie, and as a result, even when God gave me wonderful blessings, like a beautiful wife and beautiful daughter, I didn't see it that way. In fact, I took them for granted. I hurt them in the worst way. My wife at the time was a believer in Christ, and I mocked her. I realize today that the Lord had been chasing me down my whole life, but my own free will always got in the way. He sent me a beautiful, God-fearing woman, and I tossed her away like garbage. I have also done some terrible things, yet here I stand, still alive. I should be six feet under today. A man stabbed me ten times in my stomach. When that happened to me, I saw a bright light. I kept talking in my mind, asking God to give me one more chance and begging that if He saved me, I would try and finally make things right. Gentleman, that was the very first time in my entire life, I had spoken to the Lord. So I stand here before you today to let you know that no matter what you've done, God still loves you. All you need to do is to ask for His forgiveness, and He will give it to you easily and freely. Accept

Jesus as your Lord, and your life will never be like it was before. Take it from me. Did I ever think I would be here talking to a bunch of young men, such as yourselves, about God? No way. If someone had predicted this future to me, I would have laughed in their face. I'm here for open discussion. I'll answer any questions or hear your comments. Ask me anything, and I will answer your questions the best way I can."

The two acres of beautiful green pastures were accompanied by an array of red and purple morning-glory flowers. There were two beautiful twin toddlers with dirty-blond hair, one wearing ponytails and the other wearing a fluffy purple headband. They ran across the field, as happy as can be. They were being chased by their two older siblings. Their mother sat at the porch, watching her four daughters play. She could see her husband's car from a short distance approaching. The girls took notice of their daddy finally getting home from work. As soon as he stepped out of his car, they ran as quickly as they could toward him.

"Daddy! Daddy! Daddy! Daddy!" they all cried out simultaneously.

His face lit up, and he began to laugh as he opened up his arms to catch them.

"Sarah, Diana, Rachel, Ruth! How are my four beautiful girls?" John's face glimmered with joy.

Their mother, Melissa, walked toward them.

"Group hug, girls. We love you, Daddy." Melissa looked into John's eyes as she spoke.

"How's my first-grade detective husband doing today?" Melissa asked as she hugged him tightly.

"I'm doing much better now that I'm with my five beautiful girls."

Spunky Diana, who was then seven years old, spoke up. "Daddy, I want to be a detective just like you when I grow up!"

John chuckled. He said, "Aw, Diana, you could be whatever you want to be. But why do you want to be a detective like me?"

"I want to save people just like you do, Daddy." Diana held his hand. "Tag! You're it! Bet you can't catch me!"

John ran after her. Then Sarah ran up behind him and jumped on his back as she laughed so hard. John purposely fell in the grass. Now his three-year-old twins jumped up on top of him as all four girls tried tickling him.

"Okay! Okay! You win!" John laughed so hard that his belly hurt.

Melissa sat back in awe as she watched her family, blessed, happy, and whole. Seven years ago, it looked like Diana wouldn't ever get to live this wonderful life she'd had so far. It was a rough first year of her life, but with God's grace, she made it through. Not only was she 100 percent healthy, but she was considered highly intelligent and gifted. This was truly a miracle. Sarah, who was now eight years old, had no idea what Diana had gone through. She was too little to remember. Sarah loved her younger sisters; she was the nurturer of the four. Little Rachel and Ruth were complete opposites. Rachel was the entertainer; she was a ham. Ruth was the shy yet artistic one. One day, when Melissa's two older daughters grew old enough to understand, she planned on talking with them about their father. Although she never said it out loud or to anyone, Melissa had forgiven Raymond in her heart. It took a couple of years before she could do that, but once she did, a huge burden had been lifted.

The correctional officer walked into the prison library, looking for Pastor Perez.

"Pastor?"

"Yes. I'm here," Raymond said.

"You have a visitor," the correctional officer said.

"Oh? No one has notified me that they would be visiting me today. But okay. Let's go." Raymond followed him.

"You know the drill, Pastor. I'm sorry I gotta put these cuffs on you," the correctional officer said.

"No problem. You're doing your job," Raymond said while he was being cuffed.

Raymond entered the room, which was filled with several people. He saw other fellow inmates with their families or friends. He looked around the room to see who had come there to visit him. He noticed a woman with blond hair and pretty red-framed glasses who had her eyes glued on him. She stood there with a smile. He knew her from somewhere.

"Raymond?" the woman asked.

"Oh wow, Diamond!" Raymond said, surprised.

"No, please. It's Donna," she said.

Raymond hugged her. The last time he had seen her was in court when he pleaded guilty.

"Donna, it's so good to see you. What are you doing here?" Raymond asked.

"I wanted to see how you were doing. I heard through the grapevine that you got your degree while in here and that you're ministering to the inmates," Donna said. "I'm ministering at my church to the youth. I also started a foundation for runaway teens."

"That's great, Donna. Yes. My life is totally different, in a good way. Ironically, I'll be in here for a long time, but I'm at peace. I've been given a second chance. I couldn't picture doing anything else, Dia—I mean, Donna. I'm happy to see you too, because I never had the chance to tell you that I'm sorry. I was a fool and a completely different man when you met me several years ago."

"Raymond, it's okay. I made peace with my past. I had

forgiven you and Mike a long time ago. I'm not here for that. I'm just curious about something," she said.

"What's that?" Raymond asked.

"Have you spoken with Melissa at all or written her?"

"Oh no, absolutely not. I don't expect for Melissa to ever want anything to do with me. I nearly killed her and our baby." Raymond's eyes welled up as the tears made their way down his face. "That will be the biggest regret of my life," he somberly said.

"Raymond, you are a man of God now. You said it yourself; you've been given a second chance. Melissa is a faithful woman. You won't ever feel complete peace if you don't try to put your past to closure," Donna explained.

"What are you trying to tell me, Donna?"

"What I'm saying is, write Melissa a letter. Tell her how you've been saved. Tell her that you're sorry. I don't personally know her, but if she's a woman in Christ, I know she'll forgive you if she hasn't already," Donna said.

Raymond stood up and moved over to hug her.

"Thank you, Donna. You're right. I'm going to write her an apology letter."

Hours had passed. Raymond sat in his cell with a pen and a piece of paper. He began writing. He wrote and wrote some more. He realized at that moment that the little boy he used to be, who had been battered for most of his childhood, grew up and in turn battered someone he should have loved. He received clarity that sometimes hurt people hurt other people. After completing his letter to Melissa, Raymond already felt closure in his heart. Something told him forgiveness was on its way back to him.

A NOTE FROM THE AUTHOR

Dear Friends,

I prayed for God to guide me as I wrote each and every chapter of my first novel. God has allowed me to have trials and victories in my own life that inspired me to write this story. This is a story that we can probably all relate to regardless of whether you've ever been a victim of domestic violence. First, I would like to emphasize that it is never okay to be abused in any way. There is no excuse. Sometimes the person who inflicts pain on someone else, at one point, may have been a victim him- or herself. As I mentioned at the end of my story, hurt people tend to hurt other people. It's just not an easy topic. We each, individually, face different kinds of troubles, trials, and problems in one way or another. Sometimes, we suffer because we made the wrong choices and didn't recognize the guidance of the Lord; sometimes, we suffer as a testing of our faith. Other times, we suffer merely as a grievous and unfortunate result of the evil in the world. Some of us may have a past that we're ashamed of, and we feel that there's no way God can accept us. In 1 Peter 5:10 (NIV), the Bible says, "And the God of all grace, who called you to his eternal glory in Christ, after you have suffered a little while, will himself restore you and make you strong, firm and steadfast."

God never said that weapons wouldn't be formed against us, but He does promise that they will not prosper, as said in Isaiah 54:17. In my own life, I've dealt with some really difficult situations, and as I have grown older, I've looked all around me and witnessed people like family, friends, or even strangers who have gone through hardships and situations that have crushed their spirits.

The devil's main strategy is an attempt to fill our minds with lies through our sufferings, to distract us and get us off track from God's purpose and will for our lives. It's happened to me many times. I choose to believe the promises that God has in store for me, trusting in God's word. God's word is the truth and the good news. The good news is that Jesus Christ, our Lord, sacrificed His life to wipe away our sin. He defeated the devil at the cross. He freed us from condemnation. We've been given the gift of salvation. So many people live their whole lives never fulfilling what God had in store for them. Why? I think because they believe the enemy's lies instead of standing strong, working, and pushing toward the truth and victory. The enemy fills your head with lies such as the following:

- You're not good enough.
- You're not smart enough.
- You're not strong enough.
- Do you really think you can do this?
- You don't have time for this.
- You've already made too many mistakes.
- You're a nobody.
- Who are you anyway?
- It's too late for you.
- You're damaged goods.
- Nothing good ever happens to you.

- You're out of luck.

On the topic of suffering, has your suffering been as a result of someone who hurt you? Someone who inflicted pain upon you, whether that pain was physical, emotional, mental, or spiritual? I can speak for myself, having been hurt by people close to me. Does that warrant unforgiveness toward them? Do they deserve forgiveness? Truth is if we don't forgive others, God can't forgive us either. I've wrestled with this fact for many years. How could I forgive someone who caused me so much pain? But I've also wrestled with the question, how would I feel if God didn't forgive me for my sins or mistakes? At the end of the day, we all are with sin, yet God still offers us the gift of grace. Over time, I learned that no matter how badly someone had hurt me, when I forgave him or her, it freed me from any bitterness in my own heart. In fact, for me, forgiving someone begins the healing process in my own life. It's real freedom. And it actually brings me immense peace. As it is said in Matthew 6:14–15 (NIV), the Bible says, "For if you forgive other people when they sin against you, your heavenly Father will also forgive you. But if you do not forgive others their sins, your Father will not forgive your sins."

Jesus Christ was doubted, mocked, betrayed, rejected, humiliated, laughed at, spat at, lashed, scourged, nailed to the cross, and crucified. When He rose from the dead, did He come back with a vengeance for those who hurt him? No. He came back with unconditional love, forgiveness, and grace in His heart for us, especially for those who hurt Him. So when I think of that, I do my best to exercise forgiveness more easily and leave the past where it belongs. Is it easy to do that? Absolutely not, in fact, it's really hard. But I now understand how much God's love is for me, because I've also done things to hurt and disappoint Him, yet when I'm sorry, He still forgives and accepts me.

I pray for and encourage you. No matter what pains you've been through, God is there with you every step of the way. I pray for healing of any spiritual, mental, emotional, or physical wounds that have been inflicted on you. I pray for us to learn and exercise forgiveness more easily and bind any bitterness, unforgiveness, sadness, or negative feelings away from our hearts. And for those who may not feel worthy of forgiveness because you've done too many bad things, well, that's the amazing beauty of what Jesus did for us by sacrificing Himself. He took our burdens, and in turn, we are redeemed by His blood. Redemption is offered to all of us, if we only accept Jesus as our Lord and accept the free gift of grace and salvation. I pray that you have a renewed hope in everything that you thought was dead, because with Jesus, there is hope for new things, new beginnings, and new dreams to become realized in your life. We need only to let go and just believe!

With love in Christ,
Tanya South

Printed in the United States
By Bookmasters